ECHO ISLAND

978-1-5359-9671-6

Published by B&H Publishing Group
Nashville, Tennessee

Dewey Decimal Classification: YF
Subject Heading: REALITY—FICTION / LIFE—FICTION /
ADVENTURE—FICTION

1 2 3 4 5 6 7 • 24 23 22 21 20

ECHO ISLAND

JARED C. WILSON

B&H
PUBLISHING

For Becky.
Thanks for waiting.

Ye suppose perchance
Us well acquainted with this place: but here,
We, as yourselves, are strangers.
—Dante, *Purgatorio*

Imagine this, I said to myself. Imagine this,
and then see what comes of it.
—Paul Auster, *Oracle Night*

CONTENTS

1

INTO THIN AIR

The four boys went camping in the state park on the mainland the weekend after their high school graduation, eating fire-cooked meals and playing cards and goofing off, assuming the entire time that the town of Echo Island would still be there when they returned.

Early Sunday, the last day of their trip, Jason George, a boy most average, emerged from the tent first, escaping the mélange of breath and feet and passed gas, sealing his friends back in with their rankness. He stretched his sore arms up toward the glowing canopy of the forest and inhaled the dewy morning of the Pacific Northwest.

When Jason was halfway through making oatmeal for the group, Jason's closest friend, Archer Baucus, exited and joined him by the fire, rubbing his sticklike forearms for warmth and repeatedly snorting through his hooked nose.

"Man, it's cold," Archer said. "You sleep okay last night?"

"Eh. Okay."

"I couldn't sleep at all," Archer said. "Can't get comfortable."

"You're too bony maybe."

Archer *was* bony. He was tall and stick thin, all angles and points. "Yeah, well," he said, without finishing the thought.

Jason opened another packet of plain oatmeal and poured it into a pot, adding water.

Archer poked their fire with a branch. "I don't know how Bradley can sleep in there with the way Tim snores," he said, pointing the branch at their friends' tent, still zippered.

"Tim says they're gonna room together in college, assuming Tim can get a scholarship to play ball. I think he'll shrivel up and die if he has to go somewhere Bradley isn't."

Archer shrugged. "We all used to feel that way. But then we had to grow up."

"Yeah, maybe."

"I meant to ask you last night. Are you still thinking about Washington State?"

"I think it's too late. I don't know. I have no idea what I'm going to do." Jason looked out at the trees, as if the answer to his academic future might conveniently be found there.

"I'm sure you still have time," Archer said. But he didn't sound convincing.

"If we all still played football, we could just ride on Bradley's back like Tim."

"I'm glad those days are long gone," Archer said.

They heard a rustling in their friends' tent, and the tousled blond hair of Bradley Hershon emerged.

Bradley joined them, clad only in plaid boxer shorts and flip-flops, a pale Adonis posing by the flames. He seemed unaffected by the early summer chill.

"Dude, what are you doing?" he asked.

"Making breakfast," Jason said as if it should be obvious.

"Oatmeal? Man, Jason, you are the most boring dude ever."

"I'm sorry I didn't have room to pack the hibachi," Jason said.

"I was hankerin' for eggs benedict," joked Bradley. He hocked a loogie and spit into the fire. "Archway, you got any more of those energy drinks?"

"Fresh out," said Archer.

Bradley stuck out his bottom lip in a feigned pout.

"I'm not sure we wanna see you hopped up on any more energy drinks," said Jason.

Bradley lumbered maniacally over to Jason and elbowed him in the shoulder. "You don't want me to Hulk out, young sir?"

Jason pretended to find Bradley funny. "Definitely not. Hey, man, stop. You're gonna make me knock over the oatmeal."

Bradley backed off. A rustling behind him made him turn around.

The fourth camper, Tim Cooper, a meek, pudgy, butt-of-jokes sort of boy, completed the fellowship, as Tim was never far behind Bradley.

"Did somebody say eggs benedict?" Tim said.

"Listen to this guy," said Bradley. "Class of 2002's finest. No, man, it's porridge."

Jason stopped stirring. "So, don't eat it. Whatever."

"All right, dude," Bradley said. "Don't get all chicky on me. We'll eat oatmeal. Won't we, Timmy?"

"Yeah, sure."

"Oatmeal's good for pooping."

Tim chuckled.

"And maybe it'll put some fat on Archway's bones."

Archer said, "Why don't you put some clothes on, man?"

"Why? Am I making you feel self-conscious?"

"More like revolted."

Bradley walked with a dramatic lope toward the tent, arms bent before him like a white gorilla. "Well, I wouldn't want you to revolt," he said. He emerged wearing a baggy pair of shorts and tank top while Jason ladled bubbling oatmeal into four bowls.

"Mmm. Prison food," said Bradley after his first bite.

"Shove it," Jason replied.

Bradley shoved Tim off his rock.

Tim squirmed back up. "You almost made me spill."

After they'd eaten and dressed, they packed their gear and loaded it in Bradley's open-top jeep.

"What're you guys doing this afternoon?" Tim asked.

"Just hanging out," said Bradley. "Come over if you want." Then turning to Jason and Archer, he said, "How about you two?"

"I think my dad wants me to help with some stuff in the yard." Jason tucked his sweatshirt into the top of his backpack.

"I guess I could hang out," Archer said. "I'll check in with my mom first."

"Whatever," said Bradley as he launched his sleeping bag into the back seat.

The red jeep was a graduation gift from Bradley's father, who happened to own the only car dealership on the island. It was Bradley's pride and joy, and for the last two years, it had been the boys' means of getting to the mainland for their annual start-of-the-summer camping trip.

The boys had been friends since playing on the peewee football team together in grade school. But time and seasons change things. As their personalities took shape into adolescence, so too did the unspoken fractures between them. Every summer since middle school, they'd kept up the camping tradition, and this was to be their last hurrah before parting ways for college.

They all hopped in the jeep and were soon speeding along the narrow, winding road out of the park.

Bradley, ever careless, pushed the jeep to fifty-five.

"Slow down, man," Archer said. "You'll get us all killed."

"No can do, Archway. I feel the need!"

"The need for speed!" Tim finished, completing the line with false cheer. Of the three passengers, he was the most terrified.

The apple-red projectile skirted the edge of the road in tight careens and pushed its cargo's luck on the straightaways. Barreling down a short, mist-laden grade, Bradley had no time to react to the doe leading its fawn across the street.

Tim screamed.

Bradley cursed.

They all braced as he braked hard and jerked the wheel to the right. The piercing pitch of skidding tires filled the woods. The deer froze and watched with incomprehension as the vehicle rushed at her and her fawn sideways. And then, they darted away, barely avoiding impact.

The jeep kept sliding perpendicular to the road. By the time Bradley had thought to correct his steering into the skid, the carriage was tipping, the left-side wheels lifting slightly off the ground.

When they touched ground again, Bradley was still braking, but the momentum proved too much. The jeep slid off the pavement at a sharp curve in the road and plunged briefly into a rocky ditch. The jolt knocked his foot off the brake. Packs flew out of the back; the ice chest opened its plastic mouth and spewed empty soda cans in a wide, rattling arc onto the rocks.

When Bradley finally sought the brake, he found the accelerator instead. He realized his mistake immediately and switched pedals, but the brief rush of gas gunned them up the far bank of the ditch and flipped them right-side down, skidding them into a tree. The hood crumbled like tin foil.

Some indiscernible hiss gushed from the engine, and the only other sound in the air was that of four boys panting heavily.

"Man," Archer whispered. He wasn't angry, just relieved.

More heavy breathing. A groan from the back seat.

The four of them hung suspended a few feet from the ground by their seatbelts.

Bradley could see Jason in the passenger seat blinking his eyes rapidly.

"You okay?" Bradley asked.

Jason looked up at him and nodded.

Bradley craned his neck. "You guys okay?"

Archer and Tim gave him looks that said no, but they both said, "Yes."

Bradley looked straight ahead. "Wow," he said. He gripped the steering wheel. "Can you believe that?" He snorted a laugh. "Man, my dad's going to kill me."

Archer said, "Justifiable homicide, if you ask me."

Bradley grinned from ear to ear. He gave Jason another look, one that bore the unmistakable mix of *I'm glad to be alive* and *Look what I did!* He said, "That. Was. Awesome."

"Awesome?" Jason said. "You're an idiot."

Archer waved his hand for attention. "Can we get out of the car now?"

They did, and only Tim needed assistance.

Standing in the ferny grass on the hill above the wreck, they surveyed the damage. The jeep looked so much smaller that way, like a gigantic toy tossed aside.

"I guess we should call somebody," Jason said.

"Yeah, okay." Bradley dug his cell phone out of his pocket. "Battery's dead."

"You didn't charge it?"

"Charge it in what? The fire? Tim's ginormous stomach?"

"My stomach's not ginormous."

"Eh," Bradley said. "No . . . I didn't bring a battery pack."

Jason said, "You could've charged it in the car."

"I don't think I have the, uh, little thingy," Bradley said, and he was making a stretched-line motion with his hands. "I charged it before we left. But it must've run down."

Archer said, "Tim, you got yours?"

"Yeah, I think so." Tim retrieved his phone, now a shattered black brick.

Jason looked ruefully at the jeep. Steam escaped from the edges of the crumpled hood and commingled with the dissipating morning fog.

"So, I guess we're hoofing it."

Bradley groaned. "Wait, let me check the glove compartment for my cord."

He circumnavigated the wreckage and crouched by the upturned passenger seat to remove a charger cable from the glove compartment. He plugged one end into the car's lighter and then snapped the other end into the phone.

He stared at it a few seconds. "No juice," he shrugged.

"Yeah," Jason said. "Your car is broken."

Bradley smirked. "Oh, is it?"

Archer and Tim collected the backpacks.

Bradley said, "Well, ramblers, let's get rambling."

They walked for three miles along the park road with Tim lagging behind. The trek was long and monotonous. They had covered two more miles when the urgent wail of a siren cut through the air.

"Is that behind or in front?" Bradley asked.

"Can't tell," said Jason.

Eventually, an ambulance broke into view and zoomed past, apparently oblivious to the four boys on the side of the road.

"Dude, what a jerk," said Bradley. "He flew right by us."

"Maybe he's going somewhere else," Jason said.

"That'd be quite a co-inky-dink, don't you think?"

"Maybe."

Tim said, "Maybe he just didn't see us."

"Oh, you think?" said Bradley.

"Should we go back in case they're headed to the campground?" Jason asked.

Bradley said, "Dude, that's like ten miles!"

"It was actually about five," Archer broke in.

"Thank you, Captain Odometer."

Tim looked over his shoulder, feigning consideration. Backtracking didn't appeal to him at all.

It didn't appeal to the others either.

Archer said, "When they see we're not there, they'll come back this way."

"We're closer to the pier now anyway," Bradley added. "Let's just get to the pier and take the ferry back, and I'll get my dad to take care of the car."

"Are you sure?" Jason asked.

"Yeah. There's no sense in waiting around. I can sort it out from home."

Tim said, "The Mariners are playing the Angels tonight."

"That's right," said Bradley. "Who wants to miss the game? So let's go."

Jason said, "The police, though. They'll be looking for us, trying to figure out what happened."

"Dude, I just said I'd get my dad to handle it."

"Yeah, but—"

"Jason!" Bradley looked around, clearly agitated. "Look, when we get back to the ferry landing, we can talk to somebody there. We can find a phone. Will that make you happy?"

"Yes," Jason said.

"So, losers, are we walking or not?"

They carried on then, but when they reached the pier, they found it vacant.

"Is there some sort of holiday I forgot about?" Bradley asked.

"If there was," said Archer, "everyone would be in the park."

"Dude, then, where'd everybody go?"

"How should I know? Church?"

"Lucky us; we missed the Echo Island revival."

Jason found the tiny office building empty as well. And no workers occupied the machine room.

Tim said, "Maybe something serious happened in the park. A fire or something. Maybe everyone's helping out."

Bradley said, "Did they just fly over us or what? We would have passed anybody going that way."

Tim said, "Oh, yeah."

Jason found an old pay phone, but there was no dial tone.

"They don't use those anymore, Jase," Bradley said. "Look, guys, let's just get back home. There's obviously nothing we can do here."

They all agreed and boarded the wide-open ferry.

They could see the greasy black head of Gerald Farmer, Echo Island ferryman for as long as the boys could remember, protruding from the seat of the elevated cabin.

"Should we say something to Mr. Farmer?" Jason asked.

"Be my guest," said Tim. "That dude freaks me out."

"Oh, he's harmless," said Jason, as he walked toward the metal steps ascending the cabin. He felt the flimsy platform sag under his weight.

When the door opened, the man swiveled slowly in his chair. But their pilot wasn't Gerald Farmer. Instead some stranger, a middle-aged man with froggy gray skin and a black skullcap snapped over his bald head, stared blankly at them.

"Oh," Jason said. "Um . . ."

The man wore a baseball jersey-style white shirt with black sleeves. Over a faded band photograph, in peeling letters, the shirt read: I SAW STYX AT THE PARADISE THEATRE.

Jason stifled a laugh. "Um, is Mr. Farmer off today?"

"Yes," the man said. He looked back out at the ocean pass.

"Oh. Okay."

He wanted to say, *We just had a car accident back in the park, and I was wondering if you had a phone or a radio that we could use to tell the police that everything's okay.* Instead, he knew home was just thirty minutes away, and the man creeped him out more than Gerald Farmer had ever creeped out Tim, so Jason simply repeated, "Okay," and exited.

Rejoining the group, he said, "Mr. Farmer's off today."

"So, who's driving?" Archer asked.

"I don't know. Some random dude."

Bradley waved at the cabin. "Hey, Some Random Dude!"

Bradley and Archer eventually eased into an argument over which actor played the best James Bond, Tim assumed the position of silent observer, and Jason hovered at the edge of the boat, resting his right knee on the rusted railing.

The gray ocean swirled in foamy green eddies off the ferry-cut ripples, the lumbering wake a minor disturbance in the bay. The waves rolled short and white and folded back into the opaque expanse. To Jason's left, the sun still hung low in the eastern sky, and the vast green woods of the Washington coast sunk lower and lower, as if recoiling from the sun in the slow inhale of the horizon.

When it thinned to an invisible line, he looked right, anticipating the imminent rise of the Echo Island coast from the western horizon. As soon as the land of one side dipped below sight, the land of the other poked into view, like the pass between them was some gigantic oceanographic teeter-totter, like each world hung in the balance of the ferry's traversable scale. One coast down, the other up. Inhale, exhale. That was how it worked, and since making this discovery, Jason had made it a secret ritual to watch this balance shift every time he'd traveled by ferry between the island and the mainland.

Like clockwork, like the tipping of that scale, the island slowly rose from the sea, taking its jagged shape of rocky beach and angular forest. Eventually, the beach ran as far east and west as he could see, and the ferry's bumpered hull gently rubbed against the concrete dock. The ferryman descended the cabin without a word, locked the vessel to the broad boat ramp, and lowered the gate, which usually withstood the passage of cars, but that morning only upheld the unloading of the foursome.

No sooner had their feet crunched the gravel in the landing's lot than the ferryman scooped the gate back up, unlatched the steel fasteners, and began chugging the ferry back out to sea.

"What's up with the hippie dude not waiting?" Bradley said.

Archer looked around. "I don't see anyone waiting to board."

"Yeah, but homeboy's supposed to wait. There's like, what, one-hour intervals or something? There's a schedule."

The whole thing bothered Jason, but he didn't say anything. He'd found the emptiness of the ferry station back on the mainland unnerving. And now the Echo Island landing was vacant too.

Archer asked him, "You gonna call your mom to come get you?"

"They're at church," Jason said. "I'll walk. How about you?"

"We'll just hitch a ride with Archway." Bradley turned to Archer. "You parked in the lot, right?"

"Yeah," Archer said. "Sure, no problem."

Jason said goodbye, slung his bag over his shoulder, and headed for home.

Only three blocks away, paranoia set in. He hadn't encountered a single person yet. Jason tried coming up with as many rational explanations as he could for why he hadn't so much as heard the *sounds* of other people—no voices, no cars, no machinery of any sort—in the typically bustling streets adjacent to the ferry landing. But no explanation would come. He tried telling himself that he was just tired, that his imagination was getting the better of him. It worked for a while, but the uneasiness nagged.

Jason passed through the close-set intersections off the town square. The landscape was a still life. In the parked cars, the waving flags, and the glint of sunlight off windows and chrome, the presence of people was suggested, but nowhere was it confirmed. He tried opening the door of the library, the post office, and the cell phone store, but he had chosen those doors in a strategy of self-reassurance, knowing he could tell himself they weren't open on Sunday mornings anyway. He only glanced into the windows of the diners and restaurants he knew should have been open and bustling with people.

Entering the bushy enclave of the Royal Garden subdivision, he finally breathed a sigh of relief to see a group of cars parked in the lot of the Lutheran church. He almost laughed at himself.

Once inside his house, Jason flipped the kitchen light switch. Nothing happened. He tried the living room. No light. Trying the hall light switch with the same result, he suddenly realized the unnerving quiet he'd experienced throughout the town was no doubt due to a power outage.

He climbed the carpeted steps to the second floor, entered his messy bedroom, and collapsed into bed, seeking the sleep that the previous night's goofing off had prevented.

Sleep never came, however, and after an hour of a restless tossing in his bed, Jason was startled by a pounding on the door.

He scrambled downstairs, pulling on his shirt.

Whoever was knocking was practically beating the door down.

"Hold on!" Jason said.

He turned the dead bolt and opened the door.

Archer, Bradley, and Tim stood on the front porch, huddled together as if for warmth, all of their faces terrified.

Bradley said, "Everybody's gone."

2
LIFELESS

What are you talking about?" Jason said.

The noonday sun lit up the neighborhood behind them with a surreal, cartoonish vividness, like a scene from a Florida postcard.

"Everybody's gone," Bradley repeated.

"Everybody who?"

"Everybody," Tim said, as if that cleared things up.

Archer pushed past them and stepped into the house. From the marble-tiled entryway, he offered a ponderous look to the sunken living room. "Are your parents home?" he asked.

"No, they're at church."

"Did you text them?"

"Why would I?"

Archer looked at him in that serious Archer way but didn't answer.

"My phone's not working anyway," Jason said.

Archer said, "Did you pass anybody on your way here?"

"No. I mean, I didn't see anybody."

"No cars? Nothing?"

"No. Wait—there are people at that church outside the subdivision."

Bradley said, "No, there aren't."

"Yes, there are," said Jason. "I saw the cars when I was walking by."

"There are cars," Bradley said, "but no people. We went in."

Tim was the only one who hadn't entered the house yet. On the stoop, arms limp at his sides, he stared straight ahead as if waiting for an invitation, as if waiting for Bradley's okay to move.

Jason said, "Tim, are you coming in?"

Tim opened his mouth to speak but seemed to get lost in response. He blinked dumbly.

"He's been freaking out since we found out," Bradley said.

Archer said, "We're all freaking out."

Jason reached out, grabbed Tim's arm, and pulled him into the house. He shut the door.

Turning to Bradley and Archer, he said, "Freaking out about what?"

Bradley was incredulous. "Dude. Everybody's gone."

"Vanished," Archer whispered.

"Even my dog's gone," Bradley said.

"Mine too," said Tim.

"That doesn't make any sense."

Bradley nodded.

Jason cracked a smile. "Is this some kind of joke?"

Archer flipped the light switch up and down. "Power's out here too, huh?" He crossed into the living room to pick up the landline phone sitting on a side table.

Bradley said, "It's not a joke, dude."

Archer held up the cordless receiver to his ear and shrugged. "Phone's dead."

"It's a cordless," Jason said. "It's out because the power's out."

"Every landline we've checked is out," said Bradley. "Everything's out! When the light wouldn't come on at the landing office, we checked some more along the way."

"Maybe it was a bad storm," Jason said.

"Do you remember it storming last night?"

"Power goes out all the time."

"Yeah, okay," Bradley mock agreed. Then he said sternly, "Where did everybody go, man?"

"Stop saying *everybody*," said Jason.

"What?"

"Stop saying *everybody*. You walked from the dock to here. It's a big island."

"So where is everybody, Jason?"

"It's a big island!"

Archer said, "Let's calm down. Let's think about this."

A screech of wood on tile made all three of them jump, and they turned to see that Tim had grown tired of standing. He sat in the entryway chair Jason's mother had found at an antique store the year before.

"He's right," Archer said, meaning Jason. "I mean, it's not a big island, but there are lots of places people could go. But, on the other hand, I can't think of a reason why everybody from this stretch would all go somewhere else."

"Everybody?" Jason said. "Did you look in every door? Look in every window?"

Bradley erupted. "No one's here, man!"

Jason abruptly started for the door, walking quickly and dramatically.

"Where are you going?" Bradley said.

As he flew past, Tim turned his head, confused.

Archer and Bradley followed Jason to the sidewalk and watched as he mounted the porch of the neighbor's house. He knocked on the door.

When no one answered, he pounded even harder.

"No one's there!" Bradley called.

Jason peered into a window, cupping his hand over his brow to shield the glare.

He marched back.

Bradley started to say, "I already told you—" but Jason passed them and approached the neighboring house on the other side, the home of the Vawters.

He knocked louder this time and waited longer.

Nothing.

"Car's in the driveway too," Bradley said.

Jason looked at him, clearly agitated. *Is Bradley enjoying this? Does he have to rub it in?*

Looking up and down the street, Jason thought about trying a few more houses, but he went back to the Vawters' maroon Honda Civic. They never locked their doors, so Jason opened the driver's side, meaning to honk the horn. The noise might bring someone outside, or at least to a window.

But the horn wouldn't sound.

He pressed harder on the steering wheel pad.

"What are you doing?" Bradley asked.

"I thought I could—" Jason said. He tried it again. Nothing.

He walked back to his own driveway and grasped the garage handle. His heart sank as the white accordion door rolled up. Both of his parents' cars, the white Chevy Lumina and the silver Buick LeSabre, still sat together on the oil-stained slab inside.

He walked back inside, his friends following close behind.

"It doesn't make sense," he said.

"You said yourself," Archer said, "it's a big island. They obviously went somewhere. We just have to find them."

"Batteries don't work," Jason said.

"The batteries in what don't work?"

"In everything," Jason said, although he instantly recognized that the test sample that he'd used to arrive at the conclusion was, relatively speaking, about the sample size his friends had used to conclude everyone on the island had vanished.

"Everything?" asked Bradley.

Archer looked around the room for battery-powered things. Most of the electronics were plugged into power they already knew was down. But Archer picked up the remote control, knowing it would prove its juice if the red light flickered. But he tried every button. The light never blinked.

"Tim," he said.

Tim didn't seem to hear.

Archer rose and walked over to him. "Let me see your keys."

Tim looked up at Archer like he'd just asked if he could borrow a kidney.

"Your keys," Archer repeated.

"Um," Tim managed to say.

Bradley helped. "In your pocket, broseph."

Archer said, "I want to look at your penlight."

Tim chewed on his lip like he had to think through the implications of the request. Finally, he stuffed his thick fingers in his jeans pocket and fished out his keys. Archer took them, twisted the tiny flashlight both ways, and illuminated nothing.

Jason said, "See? They're just dead."

"But *all* of them?" Archer asked. "That's quite a coincidence."

"All of them *in the house.*"

"Where do you keep your batteries?" Archer said. "The fresh ones."

"Kitchen drawer."

"Bradley," said Archer. "Remote."

Bradley tossed it to him as he walked to the kitchen.

After pulling the fifth drawer, Archer found the package of double-As.

"Forget the batteries, dude," Bradley called. "There are bigger fish to fry, like the fact that apparently, every living thing on Echo Island is gone."

Archer ignored him and replaced the batteries in the remote. He pushed buttons. The red light remained dead. "Okay," he said. "This is weird."

"We've established that, Sherlock." Bradley now stood in the doorway between the kitchen and living room. "Now can we go find everybody before Tim wets his pants and Jason needs a straitjacket?"

Archer said, "What?" He was still looking at the television's remote control. He finally looked back at Bradley.

"Dude?" Bradley said.

Archer swallowed. "Yeah, yeah, okay."

In the living room, Archer posited a plan.

"We need to walk the island, I guess."

"It takes a day to circle this thing," Bradley said.

"We'll split up, then: two and two. In opposite directions. And we'll meet up halfway."

"It's still a long walk."

They hadn't noticed Jason slipping out. He returned now, car keys in his fist.

"Both cars are dead," he said.

Archer looked at Bradley. "Unless you have a car that runs on your ego, we're walking."

"The Vawters have bikes," Jason said. "Mountain bikes."

"Yeah, bikes," said Bradley. "Bikes are good."

Tim hadn't joined them in the living room, and they hadn't felt compelled to ask him, but suddenly he piped up from his lonely spot in the sunlit foyer. "We're splitting up?"

"Yeah," Archer said. "We'll go faster that way."

Tim said, "I'm not sure that's a good idea."

"Why?"

Tim just blinked.

Jason said, "He might be right. We don't know what happened. Maybe we should stick together. For protection or something. What if we get halfway round and the other two have disappeared too? If someone gets hurt or lost, what then?"

"It just makes sense this way," Archer said. "Otherwise we'd be walking all night."

"Pedaling," corrected Tim.

"Whatever."

"What happens if we run into trouble?" Jason said. "How would the other two find out?"

"I'm not sure that's a rational fear," said Archer. "But if there's someone else, some others in the town who pose a threat, they've already managed to make five thousand people disappear, so I doubt four more would be a big deal. This way, if two of us get captured, at least there are two left to rescue them or go find help."

"Go for help," Jason said. "Why didn't we think of that? The ferry!"

"What about it?"

"It has to come back. Let's just go back to the mainland."

Bradley said, "Dude, the ferry's not coming back."

"You don't know that."

"I have to agree with Bradley," said Archer. "Mr. Farmer wasn't the pilot. And the way the hippie dude hightailed it back right after dropping us . . ."

"Maybe the ferryman's part of the operation," Bradley said.

Jason glared. "The operation? What bad movie did you climb out of?"

"A better question, I think," Archer said, "is what bad movie did we crawl *into*?" He could sense the frustration building in Jason, so he added, "Okay, look—one of us can start back at the ferry landing. Wait an hour. See if it returns."

Jason wasn't appeased, but Archer continued anyway.

"Also, probably not a bad idea to check our phones every now and then. And see if any cars have keys left in them. Check the insides of big buildings like schools, the Catholic Church on Granger Road, the stadium, the movie theater, you know?"

"Yeah, yeah," said Bradley. "Let's go."

"All right," Archer said. "Who's with who?"

Tim again broke in. "I'll go with Bradley."

Bradley sat up straight and contemplated the still figure of his friend in the entryway. "You gonna be okay, Biggie Smalls?"

Tim's brow furrowed. "What?"

"You're not gonna, like, freak out on me or anything?"

"I don't think so."

Bradley frowned. He said to Archer and Jason, "Yeah, I'll take Tim. But who's going where?"

"It doesn't matter," Archer said.

"You're the smart guy," said Bradley. "You tell us."

Archer chewed his lip for a second, then said, "Jason and I will go east. Lots of room there for people to congregate. We can check the stadium, for instance. You guys start at the ferry station and head up the western coast from there."

They liberated four bicycles from the Vawter family's garage and set out, two and two down Royal Garden Drive and then in opposite directions on Steeplechase at the mouth of the subdivision.

Bradley and Tim pedaled right and then south to the ferry landing, while Archer and Jason began their tour of the island's eastern side, all of them eager to find someone, anyone, on the island, and none of them prepared for what they couldn't know was coming.

3
LOOKING

Jason and Archer swerved around the gentle slopes of the island's uneven terrain. Since he'd been a kid, the short, soft grasses of the town, running in low mounds and sunlit patches around the narrow streets, had always reminded Jason of a mini-golf course, a life-size replica of a tiny prefab landscape. He'd traveled around the island all his life, but this day felt different, *looked* different. The midday sun shone perceptible edges. It gave off the same light and warmth, but it was a cartoon sun all of a sudden, and the windless air only added to the eerie quality of their exploration.

The disappearance of the townspeople changed the town itself, the way his empty and powerless house suddenly felt like a stage set. Or maybe it was just his mind playing tricks on him.

Archer nudged his way in front of him as the right shoulder of their curve dropped off. He followed the trajectory of a battered guardrail to the halfway point and skidded slowly to a stop.

"What's wrong?" Jason asked.

"You know what's down there?"

Archer pointed his bony finger down the slope and into the dense forest on the other side of a rocky ditch about forty yards away.

"What?" Jason asked.

Archer then pointed up, and Jason lifted his gaze to the thick mass of power lines running overhead. Behind the boys, the lines stretched to a steel tower and continued their journey out of sight; before them, the lines slanted down over the forest to the invisible shoreline.

"The power station's down that ridge," Archer said.

"So what?"

"Maybe we can find out what happened to the power. A downed line or something. Maybe lightning struck."

"Do you know how to fix stuff like that?"

"Well, no."

"Then what's the point?" Jason asked. "We're supposed to cover the island looking for everybody. It'll take two days if we keep stopping to look at everything."

"I'm just trying to figure out what's going on," Archer said.

"I know. But the best way to figure that out, I think, is to find everybody."

"Okay, then let's check the beach first."

"We can see it best from the rise," said Jason, nodding at the fork in the road at the end of the curve. To the right, the pavement rose steeply and opened out next to a rest area with one of the island's best panoramic ocean views.

Pedaling up the hill proved grueling, and Archer gave up halfway, dismounting and walking the bike up the rest of the slope. Jason dropped from his bike too and followed.

When they reached the slice of land holding three picnic tables and two barbecue grills, they leaned the bikes against the fence and walked to the wood railing along the grassy cliff. Over the emerald fans of conifer and spruce, the gray ripple of the shore ran empty as far as they could see in either direction, the only movement the lapping of the surf.

The boys both stared in silent disappointment. There were no signs of life.

Jason finally said, "Keep going, I guess."

Archer agreed, and they resumed the search.

Tim lagged behind Bradley throughout the straight-shot trek to the ferry landing. They cut through the commercial district that bordered the western coast of the island. Bradley banged on every car with an alarm sticker in its window, just to check Archer's battery theory, but no alarms sounded.

There had to be a logical explanation for everything, but Bradley always had trouble with logic. Every mystery movie, even the terrible and terribly obvious ones, seemed good to him; he could never guess whodunit even while others laughed at how ludicrously telegraphed the solution had been. And *this*—this vanishing of the town—did not easily provoke any solution in his mind.

They rolled onto the gravel lot of the landing, and Tim abruptly said, "Maybe it was the rapture."

"What?"

"You know, the rapture. Jesus came back and took everyone to heaven."

Bradley felt like smacking him. "The rapture? Did Jesus just forget about *us*?"

"We weren't on the island."

"So, Jesus just raptured the island?"

Tim thought about that for a second. He hated when Bradley got into retort mode, which seemed like all the time.

"Okay," Tim finally said. "We got left behind because . . . you know."

"What?" Bradley said.

"Well, Jesus doesn't take everybody. Didn't you read *Left Behind*?"

Bradley didn't really read books. "No. Did you?"

"Well, no," said Tim, "but I know He doesn't just take anybody, supposedly."

"But we go to church."

"Yeah," said Tim uneasily.

Bradley added, "Sometimes, I mean."

Tim looked at him.

"All right, I see what you're saying," Bradley said. "But what about Jason? He's a Christian, right? Why didn't Jesus take *him*?"

"You never can tell."

"Nah. The dude's a straight-up dork for Jesus. More than any of us are, anyway. If he didn't make the cut, something's seriously screwed up with the rapture vacuum if it sucked up the whole town but not him."

Tim thought about that. "Yeah, I see what you're saying."

"It's not the rapture," said Bradley, but his eyes read hope more than assurance.

"Then what is it?"

"Dude! That's what we're trying to find out."

At the ferry landing, Bradley dismounted the bike and didn't bother with the kickstand, letting it fall to the ground. While Tim tried getting his stand to lodge in the gravel, Bradley walked to the concrete dock. As if some clue might await him, he peered cautiously over the edge to see the slosh of the brackish water against the rubber brace. He muttered to himself, "Man, we shoulda known something was up when it wasn't Mr. Farmer driving the ferry."

As Tim came to replicate Bradley's downward gaze into the water, Bradley walked between the deep ruts formed by countless cars, heading for the machine room. It was a long, rickety, garage-like building with one half hovering on decks over the water so boats could be brought in.

Bradley had been in the machine room once before, when he was eleven years old and curious. He still remembered the blast of noise that assaulted his adolescent ears when he opened the metal door, the sounds of cranks and air-powered tools, the blare of grunge rock on a boom box, and the conversational shouting of the same two or three workmen who seemed to always be there. As a kid, he found it disorienting and impressive.

Now when Bradley opened the door, the only sound was the ambient hush and trickle of water. He wasn't sure what he expected to see. A crew of evil henchmen, perhaps, or a gang of terrorists holding people hostage. But not nothing.

The boom box, upgraded since the midnineties of course, still sat on the paint-splattered table to his right. Bradley tried turning it on. No juice.

Tim's face appeared over his shoulder. "What's in here?"

"It's the, uh, what you call it? Repair . . . place."

Tim skirted the narrow boat ramps.

"Be careful, dude," Bradley said.

Tim didn't respond, but he walked the length of the structure, peering behind crates and around huge pulley contraptions. At the far end, a motorboat with its tail in the water was lashed to a rusty hook in the concrete floor.

"We could take the boat," he said.

"What do you mean?"

"I don't know," Tim said. "Around the island. Back to the mainland. Whatever. It'd be faster than the bikes."

Bradley frowned at him, but he thought it wasn't an entirely bad idea. Of course, they couldn't explore ground in the boat. But if the entire population of the town was near any of the coasts, they could spot them much sooner than they could traveling by land. And getting back to the mainland sounded good too. If something really bad had happened, they'd want to contact the state police.

A phone sat next to the radio, and he picked it up. No dial tone.

"Yeah, let's try the boat," he said.

Despite some difficulty involving a complicated latch and Tim almost falling into the water, they managed to raise the large door to the ramp. They slid the boat down into the water until it floated, and while Tim stood on the cement walkway still holding the rope, Bradley sat in the vessel trying to start the motor.

But it was no use. The thing had gas. The sparkplugs even looked new. But as hard as Bradley yanked on the starter, nothing happened. He had started several identical boats hundreds of times in his short life as an amateur sailor, so he knew what he was doing.

But nothing worked.

"Pull it over, so I can climb out," Bradley said.

They checked the office again, where both of them pushed buttons, flicked switches, and listened to receivers to no avail.

After a silent final survey of the ocean pass between themselves and the invisible west coast of Washington, they remounted their bikes and, taking a left out of the parking lot, headed south to resume the investigation.

"Shouldn't we wait to see if the ferry comes?" Tim huffed.

"It's not coming back, dude," said Bradley.

Tim didn't argue.

The padlock on the Echo Island High School stadium gate was secure. Archer pondered the concertina wire adorning the tall chain-link fence.

"Think we should try it?" Jason asked.

"I don't know. The stadium would be the perfect place to keep everyone. It's one of the only places big enough. But unless they're all bound and gagged, it seems like thousands of people would make some kind of noise."

Jason jogged along the fence to where it ended at a rocky cliff face.

"You can't squeeze through there," Archer called.

"Not squeezin', just lookin'."

From his vantage point against the barrier, Jason could see right through the open gate into the stadium. He could see the end zone and almost half of the field.

"Can you see?" Archer asked.

"Yeah. Unless they're sitting utterly silent in the stands, they're not in there."

When Jason returned, Archer said, "The question now is, do we keep going north to the lighthouse or cut inland and check the theater?"

"Makes sense to move in and work our way out, right?"

"Yeah. But if everyone's on a boat or something headed out to sea, the longer we wait, the longer they have to get out of sight."

"Even if everyone left, don't you think they'd leave a note? A sign? Something?"

"Yes," Archer said. "Unless they didn't leave by choice."

"Five thousand people, man. You can't kidnap five thousand people without leaving a trace."

Archer said nothing, but his face said, *I'm not dumb.* He was capable of doing the math.

Archer was now in one of his dazes. Jason punched him lightly on the arm.

Archer blinked several times fast. "Sorry, I can't help it," he said.

Jason smirked, nodded. "So, the lighthouse."

"I think we should cover the island and then start testing theories if we don't find them."

Jason said, "It's just weird."

"I know."

"Are you scared?"

"Nervous," said Archer, "if that's what you mean. I try not to be scared of things until I know what it is exactly that I should be scared of."

"But your mom. My mom and dad. My brother."

"We may find them. They're not gone until we can't find them anywhere, and we're not done looking."

"So, the lighthouse," Jason said again.

"The lighthouse."

Four miles north of the stadium—at the end of a straight and gradually rising road lined with thin cedars—the pinnacle of a lush, windswept promontory, the pocked and weather-mottled Echo Island lighthouse resembled the discarded bone of some gigantic prehistoric beast.

The boys found the door open. The tiny elevator didn't work, so they climbed the shaky spiral staircase to the lookout and scanned the oceanic horizon. The Pacific was the same as it had ever been, azure and gray and churning from the eternal, unseen disturbance, but it was void of ship or sign. One could always spot an array of fishing boats on the water from the lighthouse, but not today. Far to the east an ominous array of storm clouds obscured their view of the mainland.

Jason kept looking, hoping, while Archer played with the computer and radio equipment.

"Anything?" Archer asked.

"Nothing," said Jason. "How about you?"

"Everything's dead."

Jason circled the parapet, looking back over the island itself.

"Man, this is biza—"

Archer looked up. "What is it?"

"C'mere, dude."

Archer's eyes followed Jason's pointing finger across the thick woods cradling the western coast. Miles and miles away, into the sky he seemed to be pointing.

"See that?"

"What?"

"Right there, in that sorta corner. Look right above the trees. Do you see it?"

"I do."

In the hazy distance, a thin line of smoke was rising from the forest.

"That's a chimney fire," Archer said.

Jason was already starting for the stairs. "Well, come on."

"I need a rest, man."

Tim practically tumbled off his bike, dismounting clumsily and ambling for the corner bus stop, where he fell onto the bench.

Bradley knew Tim had been sucking wind for five miles, but he hoped he could tough it out. They'd already investigated two churches, two convenience stores, and the bus station, and Bradley thought they were making good time on their appointed rounds. He considered his huffing friend only a mild irritation. He was used to such breakdowns.

"That other church is only a couple more miles up the road," he said. "And the Bee Market. Want me to go and come back?"

"No," Tim said a little too loudly.

"All right, dude. I'll wait for you."

Bradley tried popping a wheelie but couldn't. He left the bike in the street and joined Tim.

"Scoot over, wheezie."

The thick sweat on Tim's face glistened in the sunlight. He was nearly hyperventilating.

"Geez, calm down, dude. It's going to be okay."

Bradley weakly patted Tim's damp back.

Tim started to cry.

Bradley sighed. "Man, don't do that." He put his hand on Tim's shoulder. "It'll be okay. We'll find them."

"Where?" Tim said. "Where did they go?"

"I don't know."

"I'll never see my parents again."

"Don't say that."

"Aren't you freaked out?"

"It's freaky," Bradley said. "I'll admit that. So yeah, I'm freaked out. But, come on, we don't know what's going on. I'm sure there's a good explanation for this."

A moment later, Tim asked, "Hey, do you remember when you hit Clarence Deakins?"

"Huh? What are you talking about?"

"When you punched Clarence," Tim said.

"What's that got to do with anything?"

"That was cuz of me, right?"

"What? No."

"He was going to complain to Coach about me being on the team. Cuz his cousin got cut, and he thought I sucked. He thought I was only on the team because I knew you, and cuz your dad and Coach were friends."

"*Are* friends."

"*Are* friends, right. But yeah, is that why you got in a fight with him?"

"Dude, I barely remember that."

"It was the beginning of last year," Tim said.

"Why are you asking me this right now?"

"Just answer me. Did you hit him cuz of me?"

"Dude, Clarence Deakins is an idiot. I popped him cuz he deserved it, cuz he deserved it just for being Clarence."

"But why'd you stick up for me?"

"I don't know," Bradley shifted uncomfortably before standing up. "Come on, man. Time's wastin'."

As they started for their bikes, Bradley abruptly stopped.

"What?" Tim said.

Bradley stared at a red metal box next to the bench.

"The newspaper," he said.

"Yeah?"

"It's today's date."

"So . . ."

"We were only gone two nights. So, whatever happened to everybody happened late last night or early this morning." Bradley went on. "What time you think they print the next day's paper? What time you think they put them out?"

"I dunno. Early."

"So, whatever happened probably happened today. This morning, before we got back."

4

WANDERING

Hey, maybe there's a clue in there," Tim said.

"In where?"

"The newspaper. Get one out. Maybe there's a weather report or news story that can help us figure this out."

"Maybe," said Bradley.

He pulled the handle on the machine, and it didn't give.

"Got a dollar in change?"

"No."

Bradley said, "Hmm," as he looked up and down the street.

"What are you looking f—" Tim started to say, but before he could finish, Bradley started yanking on the handle with great, rattling force.

"Whoa, what're you doing?"

Bradley stopped, looking at him dumbly. "Getting a paper, what's it look like I'm doing?"

"You're gonna break it."

"Right," said Bradley, and he shook his head in aggravation and resumed jerking on the machine. When he couldn't get the lock to snap, he started kicking the plexiglass window on the front.

Tim yelled, "We can just get one off somebody's driveway." But Bradley ignored him. Kicking the newspaper machine wasn't just practical; it was cathartic.

Tim didn't like the look on Bradley's face. It was one he'd only seen two or three times in his life. It was the look Bradley got whenever reason and patience became unintelligible to him and violence became its own logic.

The translucent window proved tough. Before he could even break it, Bradley managed to kick the machine on its back.

"You're gonna hurt yourself," Tim said.

Bradley stood over the fallen contraption and started ramming the heel of his foot down into the facing. Eventually, it cracked and, after a few more slams, split open.

They divided the paper up and sat on the bench, scanning the headlines for anything that might begin to explain their predicament.

Tim first pondered the date on each turned page, as if it might say something to him, as if it might convey some sense of its own significance. Less speculative, Bradley scanned quickly, looking for keywords in bold print without expecting anything really.

The world, national, and entertainment news revealed nothing. The local news consisted of school board items, park reports, and updates on native personalities. This section was as thin as Echo Island was uneventful, which is to say *very*. There was no news about storm drills or any major event that might attract most of the populace. Even the weather forecast looked unremarkable: clear skies, relatively calm seas, and mild temperatures. No reports of lightning storms, power outages, or anything of the sort.

Tim figured read-outs at the lighthouse weather station might be revelatory. He looked at the date again, hoping it would rearrange itself into an answer.

Bradley crumpled up the paper, chucked it into the street, and wiped the newsprint from his hands onto his shorts.

Tim said, "They couldn't have just disappeared."

"Well, okay, then," Bradley said matter-of-factly. "We should start looking again."

On the long ocean road crowning the island's western face, Jason and Archer pedaled feverishly for the south woods. Occasionally, on a rise or wide-open patch, they thought they could still see that wisp of smoke, thin as pencil lead against the blue sky that was miles in the distance. They had stopped briefly, cutting inland far enough just to check the movie theater, where they found an empty parking lot and locked doors. They decided then to leave other large buildings for later inspection and book it toward the source of the smoke. But when they reached the outskirts of Archer's neighborhood, they both slowed without a word.

Jason pulled even with Archer, who stared straight ahead like he hadn't noticed. They'd sailed past the open field bordering the back of the subdivision when Jason skidded to a stop.

Archer circled. "What's wrong?" he said.

Jason cocked his head. "Don't you wanna check your house?"

"Why? We both know no one's there."

Jason looked at him. "Archer. I mean . . . your mom."

Archer spit on the pavement and kept circling, sticking a bony leg out to trace his short arc on the street with the toe of his sneaker.

Jason said, "I know it's unlikely. But you don't even want to check?"

Archer sighed and streamed for the shoulder opposite the lot. He jumped the curb, rambled over rocks and timber, and stopped at the railing separating the flatland from the steep slope down to the beach. The western world looked empty.

He rode back. "Sure, why not?" He blew by Jason and started across the field.

The two-story, white house was small, just big enough to accommodate Archer and his mother. Archer's dad left the family when Archer was three; his mom always said he took some job in the Alaskan wilderness, a job she never quite labeled. But Archer got a card from him on his thirteenth birthday that was postmarked Detroit.

Neither he nor his mother ever felt the need to search the man out. They shared a convenient, rationalistic pragmatism about nearly all things, and in their minds, Archer's dad had simply chosen an option more appealing to him. They never talked about it, but the silence was an easy one.

Archer traced a finger in the dirt on his mother's white Honda Civic as he rolled slowly by and up the cracked driveway. He and Jason leaned the bikes against the small, detached garage, which housed Archer's makeshift chemical lab and the remnants of every one of his mechanical experiments going back to early childhood.

They entered through the laundry room and navigated two baskets of dirty clothes and stacks of books that the house could no longer contain in any orderly fashion. The Baucus home was stuffed with teetering columns of books. Archer's mom taught junior high mathematics, and Archer's general interest was science, but their shared and insatiable thirst for knowledge knew no bounds.

Books about small engine repair covered the kitchen counter, theoretical physics adorned the bathroom, guides to nations they'd never visit occupied every bedroom. Books on collecting coins, stamps, comic books, baseball cards, antique dolls, McDonald's toys, and PEZ dispensers cataloged hobbies neither had. Archer's mom maintained a particular fondness for coffee table books—fine art, portraiture, landscapes, wildlife, and pop culture. If it was big and bulky and glossy, she wanted it.

Mother and son eked out a meager existence on a schoolteacher's salary and Archer's part-time jobs repairing lawnmower equipment and tutoring classmates, and their only extravagance was books. Jason reckoned the Baucuses owned more tomes than the island's public library. (They were not nearly as organized, however.)

As they entered the dim and dusty kitchen, Jason yelled, "Mrs. Baucus?"

Archer shot him an angry look.

"What?" Jason said.

But Archer didn't explain.

He walked across the dingy linoleum and onto the ancient brown carpet of the living room, looking about suspiciously as if he expected an intruder, not his mother. He pushed the power button on the tiny television. Nothing happened.

Jason, still in the entryway between the kitchen and living room, flipped the light switch to no results either.

Archer walked robotically to the downstairs bedroom where his mother slept. He knocked, then pushed the door open. The blank digital alarm clock stared back at him from the bedside table like a black eye. She wasn't in the bathroom either.

Archer came back to the living room and plopped down in silence on the couch.

Jason said, "I'll look upstairs."

He, of course, found it unoccupied, so he sat on the couch next to Archer, resigned to waiting out his friend's mental exercise.

Archer finally said, "There has to be a logical explanation for this."

"Yeah."

"People don't just disappear. And with power out everywhere."

"Yeah, I know."

As they crossed back through the kitchen, Archer said, "Hey, are you hungry?"

"No, not really."

"Yeah, me neither." He looked at the refrigerator. "All that stuff's gonna go bad, though."

"What do you mean?"

Archer looked at him, blinking.

"Oh, right," Jason said. "Electricity."

Archer's brow furrowed, and he chewed his lips. "I keep thinking I've read something about this before, but I can't remember where."

Jason couldn't tell if he was more chagrined at not finding his mother or at not remembering some random text that might shed light on their mystery. He assumed the latter. Archer was ever the pragmatist.

"Hey, look," Archer said.

"What?"

"The clock."

Jason looked at the wall clock. "It's not ticking. Guess your batteries are shot too."

"No. I mean, yeah, that too. But look at the time. It was 8:57 when the hands stopped moving."

"Huh. I wonder if that's a.m. or p.m."

"Good question, but at least we have some roundabout digits for what time the island shut down."

There was a spark in Archer's eye now.

Jason said, "Yeah, man."

Archer scratched his narrow chin.

Jason stood. "Now let's go check out that smoke."

Tim pondered a problem in the frozen foods section of the Bee Market. All those lovely pizzas and egg rolls spoiling for lack of refrigeration.

"Dude," Bradley said, "those things have enough nitrates in them to last till World War Ten."

"It's nitrites, I think."

"Whatever. Are you hungry?"

Tim retrieved a supreme pizza and examined the ingredients.

Bradley opened a package of pizza bagels. "Pull," he said, and he began throwing them through the air, pausing after each toss to mock shooting skeet. "Ka-bow!"

Tim winced. "You're making a mess."

Bradley snorted. "I would love for the cops to come arrest me, man. But you know what? Ain't. Nobody. Here."

Tim shook his head and continued trying to parse the lesser ingredients on the pizza box.

Bradley skipped a pizza bagel off Tim's shoulder. Tim flinched but ignored it.

"Baby Huey! *Tienes hambre?*"

Tim didn't look up but said, "No, I'm not hungry."

"Well, lo and behold, miracles happen! Look, if you're not hungry, why are we hanging out here?"

"Don't you think we should get some food for later?"

"Why, you think all the grocery stores are gonna disappear too?"

"No. It's just, it's such a long walk."

"Well, I don't think our pantries got raptured. So, we can always put the walk off until we run out of whatever we got at home."

Tim nodded. He returned the pizza but removed a couple of burritos.

Bradley sighed. "I'm going over to the magazines. I think Anna Kournikova is in the new *GQ*."

"She's gross," Tim muttered.

Bradley grinned but kept walking away. "Dude, them's fightin' words, but it's too early in the day to kick your butt."

Tim had found his way past the registers to the candy machines by the front windows, and Bradley was still perusing the periodicals when a loud clang sounded from the back of the store.

Both boys froze.

Bradley's mind stalled. It took him a second to register what he'd even heard. Finally, he yelled out, "Tim?"

The reply came instantly. "Wasn't me!"

Both of them rushed to the back and met at the swivel doors by the butcher's counter, which Bradley pushed through roughly. A big aluminum pot lay on the tile next to a metal cart.

The boys looked at each other in wide-eyed wonder. Bradley put a finger to his lips to signal silence. Side by side, they crept about the long room, half of which served as storage, half of which served as the butcher's workspace. The deep space opened up into more storage, an employee breakroom, and then offices that led to a rear exit.

Bradley jogged toward it and burst out. A thin strip of pavement served as the back lot, but beyond the curb lay an embankment rising up to a curtain of trees. On either end of the store, smatterings of small businesses stood.

"Shoot," he said.

Tim caught up. "No way to tell?"

"No. Could've gone anywhere. But at least we know not everybody's gone."

"Yeah. But it could've been one of *them*."

"Who?"

"Whoever did all this."

Bradley scanned the tree line. "That's assuming," he said, "that somebody did all this. We don't know what happened. They could've been someone like us, but who's just scared."

Tim asked, "You wanna go check out the woods?" But his face indicated hope for a negative.

Bradley obliged. "I'd like to, but all we've got is a knocked-over pot and no sign of where they went. Might not have even gone into the woods, but if they did, they've got a pretty good head start on us. I say we just stick with the program."

Jason and Archer traveled south along the island's western coast, between Archer's neighborhood and the forest where they saw the smoke. The path rose and fell and wound through dense woodlands and around the town's unofficial hotel district. They passed four bed-and-breakfasts and five country inns, all of which were booked fairly steadily throughout the non-winter months with tourists seeking the romance and grandeur of Pacific Northwest island life. The boys stopped at the first two bed-and-breakfasts to snoop around, but they didn't expect to find anybody, and they didn't. After that, they bypassed the other inns, despite the abundance of cars in the small parking lots. Still, they saw no one. And as there were no large buildings left on the long stretch from the lighthouse to the southwestern woods, they beelined for the woods.

The arduous ride through the woods lasted forty-five minutes, and then they rode for thirty minutes on the bike trail that lay just inside the forest park. The far end of the park ended where the trails did—against a dense wall of trees and brush that even the rangers didn't monitor.

"There bears in there?" Jason asked.

"Probably," said Archer. "But I've never seen one. You ever seen one on the island?"

"Just once, when we were driving through the park when I was a kid. But I've never hung out in these woods either."

"I think the worst danger in these woods is probably getting lost."

"Or maybe a rabid raccoon."

Archer nodded, not registering the joke. "Come on," he said.

They laid their bicycles down and walked through the high sylvan curtain. Past the initial brushy overlay bordering the wildwoods from the bike trails, the ground ran relatively smoothly, although in a gentle upward grade. They stepped over rocks and around moss and weaved in and out of both fallen and towering trees hundreds of years older than the town.

Through juniper, oak, pine, and birch, they hiked up the wet, grassy mounds in the direction of the clear sea air. Although he was the more rugged of the two, Jason followed Archer. They weren't hiking so much as investigating, and anybody would have followed Archer's lead on such a case.

Suddenly, Archer stopped and raised his bony hand to command silence.

Jason listened. Then he whispered, "What?"

Archer didn't answer, but his face puzzled.

And then, breaking through the silence of the woods came a low, moaning roar.

When it stopped, Jason waited a beat and then said, "What was that? A whale?"

"A whale? I don't think so," Archer scoffed.

"Are we close to the water?"

"Not close enough to hear a whale."

"Another mystery to solve."

"Right," Archer chuckled. "Come on, let's keep going."

When the ridge seemed to level out, they faced denser woods. The upper boughs of the tall trees interlocked arms, darkening as they rose. Only splinters of light fell through, and the air looked hazy and vaguely golden. Every creaking branch and swirl of leaves spooked them, and they found themselves whirling about at the slightest sound.

"Do you know where you're going?" Jason said.

"Why are you whispering?"

"I don't know. We don't know who's in these woods, or who's making that fire."

Archer whispered back, "Okay. No, I don't know where I'm going. I'm not sure if we're even close to that house, or whatever it is. I'm just assuming the smoke came from a chimney, remember. But even if it is, and even if we are close to it, I hope that if somebody's there, they *will* hear us and come out. Don't you?"

"I guess," said Jason. "Unless . . . I mean, what if it's someone we don't want to meet?"

"I don't know what you've got in your head, but I really doubt terrorists or serial killers or whatever it is you're imagining would light a cozy fire to alert everyone to their location. Look, the minute we stop thinking logically about this thing is the minute we stop figuring it out."

"Whatever. Let's just keep going."

Archer resumed the lead on his improvised trail. "My plan," he said over his shoulder, "is to get to the coastline at the end of the woods and search along it. If there's a house or a ranger's station or anything else out here, it more than likely overlooks the beach."

"Makes sense," Jason said, but inside, he was begrudging Archer's customarily emotionless analytical mode.

They hiked another thirty minutes under the stifling wooden cloisters, and then, the boughs seemed to gradually open up. They could hear the ocean for fifteen minutes before they could see it, but eventually, they stood upon a rocky ledge overlooking a thirty-foot drop to the gray sands of the beach.

"There's the smoke," Archer said. And there it was indeed, trailing a thin line into the sky about two hundred yards north, the direction from which they'd come.

Jason pushed past Archer and began traipsing the perilous line between the woods and the cliff.

"Watch your step, man," Archer said.

He crept behind on his spindly legs, and eventually, they came upon a stone cottage peeking out of the forest. A picture window overlooked a panoramic view of the Pacific Ocean, but dark curtains had been drawn across it.

Archer pointed at the slate-shingled roof upon which sat a red chimney, the source of that line of smoke still listing into the air like the end of a dying cigar.

Jason led the way to the door, a large expanse of wood with a latch handle instead of a knob. "Should we go in?"

"We could knock," Archer said, reaching past him to rap on the door.

When there was no answer, they looked at each other expectantly, and Archer knocked again, much louder this time.

"Hello?" he called out.

Jason put a cheek against the window, trying to see through the gap between the drapes and the inside wall. "It's dark in there, man. I don't think anyone's home."

"Given that nobody else is home either, that's probably a safe guess."

"But the fire . . ."

Archer put his hand on the door handle.

"What are you doing?"

"What?" Archer said as he pressed the button.

The sound of the latch lifting almost made Jason jump, and before he could say anything, Archer began easing the door in.

"Hello?" he offered meekly as he opened the door wide.

In the dust-filled light from the fire and the doorway, they could see that the cabin was not exactly arranged for habitation. The place consisted of one spacious room laid out with rough, hardwood floor. One beaten leather trunk, a brick hearth at the fireplace that held a poker and spade, and a small wooden desk in the far corner occupied the space.

On the desk sat a short stack of blank paper with a black fountain pen resting diagonally on top. To the upper right of the desktop was an inkwell and to the upper left, a green ashtray with three cigarette butts.

Most curious, however, was the ramshackle wooden bookcase adjacent to the desk. Each cobwebby shelf held a row of green notebooks, all of them identical on the exterior. Archer pulled one from the bookcase. It was the sort of composition journal one might find at a high-end stationery store or in the gift section of a bookstore. He thumbed through the entire thing. Every line was filled with illegible writing. He stopped on a random page and concentrated.

"What in the world?" he muttered. He turned to Jason. "Can you read this?"

Jason took the notebook and scanned the page. "Wow. No. That's weird. Just looks like gibberish to me."

Archer put the green notebook down on the desk and took two more from the bookcase, leafing slowly through a few pages in each. "Same in these. Same handwriting. I can't read a word of it. Does that say *commitment*?"

Jason looked above Archer's fingernail. "Got me. Just looks like squiggles. Random letters. But some of these don't even look like letters. It's like a weird code or something." He slipped the notebook back into its place on the shelf. "This is like something out of a serial killer movie, man. There's got to be a hundred of these notebooks here. All filled with this gibberish."

"We don't know if it's gibberish," said Archer. "We can't read them. Doesn't mean they can't be read. They're just illegible to us."

"This isn't normal."

"Yes, I'd agree with that. But then, nothing about this day has exactly been normal."

Jason was now concentrated on the desk. "Hey, did you put that there?" asked Jason.

"Put what?"

"That ashtray. It wasn't there a second ago was it?"

"Sure it was."

"I didn't see it."

"It's kinda dark in here."

"Yeah," Jason said. He cupped his palm over the flat bowl made of dark green crystal. The three cigarette nubs garnished a gray display of their cremated bodies.

"Warm?" asked Archer.

"No."

"And that fire is practically gone. It's probably safe to say that whoever lives here disappeared with everybody else."

"So now what? Keep looking?"

Archer rubbed his chin. "Part of me wants to stay here, like maybe the gibberish writer will come back."

"But you just said you thought he disappeared too."

"Yeah, I know. But after quickly doing the math, I don't see how the fire would still be smoking this many hours after everybody left."

"You're assuming the time on the clocks is the time everyone left," Jason said.

"You're right; it's an assumption," admitted Archer. "But that chimney was giving off a fair amount of smoke earlier. That seems odd if nobody had been fueling it since early this morning."

Jason picked up one of the cigarette butts carefully between thumb and forefinger like it was a piece of crime scene evidence. He gingerly returned the specimen to the ashtray. "If you care what I think," he said, "I say we stick to the plan. Finish looking around and then meet up with the guys."

Archer cast a wan gaze over the desk. "All right," he said. But before joining Jason's retreat to the door, he removed a green notebook from the bottom of the bookcase and tucked it under his arm. "Let's go."

"What're you doing with that?"

"Don't know exactly. But it might tell us something important."

"You can't even read it."

"Not yet, I can't. But I'll figure it out."

They descended the porch, closing the door behind them.

"Probably some dude's life story. Or everything he's eaten the last forty years," said Jason.

"Or maybe," Archer said smirking, "the secrets of the universe."

"Riiight."

The two boys scrambled over the stony breach between cliff and forest, and finding their point of exit, entered the woods and the search once more.

5

WONDERING

As afternoon seeped into evening, Jason and Archer snaked slowly through tract housing, a small series of parks, and the western edge of the island's southern business district. They'd given up checking doors, content to weave on their bikes back and forth in the freedom of the abandoned streets, eyes peeled for any other signs of life. As sunlight ebbed, so too did their hopes for finding any.

They rested only once, parking themselves on the warm curb outside Meegel's Donuts, where they sat in silence and stared at their fading reflections in the Safeguard Insurance window across the road. Neither of them felt like letting the dark find them, so they stood when dusk grew gloomy and pedaled for the rendezvous point.

They could hear Bradley before they could see him. His voice boomed down Royal Garden Drive: "It's just Jason and Archway."

The duos ambled, tired and dejected, into their customary foursome.

"Tim thought you guys were everybody." Bradley poked Tim in the ribs.

"I didn't say that," Tim demurred.

"You guys see anybody?" Archer said.

"Yeah, man," said Bradley. "They're all in my pocket."

"There *are* other people here," Tim said.

"Well, wait," Bradley started.

Tim continued, "We think there was somebody else in the Bee Market. We chased him out the back and into the woods."

"We *think* he went into the woods," Bradley corrected.

A mix of hope and fear washed over Jason's face. "You saw somebody? A man?"

"No, we didn't see anybody," Bradley said. "But a pot fell in the market, and we assumed it was him. Or, I guess maybe *her*. Whoever."

"And we found a cabin with a fire," Jason said. "And some weird notebooks."

"Notebooks?"

"Oh, it's no big deal," Archer said. He didn't want Bradley and Tim pawing at his discovery until he'd had a chance to examine it closely himself. Before Jason could explain any further, Archer changed the subject: "Anything at the landing?"

"No," said Bradley. "None of the boats work either. I hope you've got some theory on all this stuff, Einstein."

"I am puzzled, definitely," said Archer. "There's got to be a logical explanation, but what I worry about is, even if we can explain it, we probably can't fix it. If you know what I mean."

"Dude, I hardly ever know what you mean."

They stopped talking for a moment, each of them staring at the ground. Finally, Archer said, "No, definitely not alone, I don't think."

In the middle of the empty street, they all suddenly felt exposed. Tim rubbed his arms like he was cold. "You think we could go inside somewhere?"

Inside his house, Jason gathered candles and lit them. His mother collected them for no apparent reason, and he had a large array to choose from.

Night hadn't darkened the house yet, but dusky dimness was overtaking it. A consortium of gray thunderheads rolled into the sky overhead.

Bradley sat on the couch cradling a pillow with a fidgety Tim next to him. Archer examined the green notebook he had brought with him, straining to make sense of the scribbles. He had a vague sense that they were in some discernible distortion, as if all he had to do was squint the right way and perfect penmanship would come into focus.

"Whatcha reading?" Bradley asked.

"Huh? Oh, just one of those notebooks I found earlier."

When Jason deemed the flickering light sufficient, he squeezed between Tim and Bradley on the couch. They sat in silence for a while until the sound of distant thunder spurred them to talk.

"What are we going to do?" Jason began.

Tim was already nodding in agreement when Bradley said, "I've got no idea." A pause. "Archway?"

The open green cover of the notebook lowered, and Archer was biting his lip.

"Any clues in that thing?" Bradley said.

"No idea," Archer said. "I can't read it. But we've discovered lots of clues, actually. No electronic functionality. The whole population gone. A few signs of life—the noise you heard in the market and the chimney smoke. We've got clues. Just no connections between them. No clear connections, anyway."

"Well, maybe if you did less reading and more thinking, you'd find some," Bradley said.

That perturbed the thinker. "Is *your* brain broken?"

Bradley smirked and looked at Jason. "Is that a trick question?"

Tim blurted, "I just really want to know what's going on!"

Bradley's smirk disappeared. "Chill out, dude. We'll figure it out."

"Everybody's gone!" Tim said. "Except there's someone else out there. And we don't know who they are or what they're after or if they want to hurt us."

"Dude! We know. Let's focus on a solution. Is that okay with you?"

Tim's eyes began to well.

"Don't do it. Dude, if you do it, I will smack you."

Jason put his back to Tim and said to Bradley, "Ease up."

Bradley shrugged.

Tim wiped his nose with his fist as Jason straightened against the back of the couch again. "Archer, is there anything you can think of that could have caused all this?"

"It depends on what the *this* is you're referring to. I can think of some scenarios that *might* explain complete electrical failure, and I can think of some that might explain the disappearance of an entire populace. But a scenario that explains both? I've got nothing."

Bradley shot the pillow like a basketball into Archer's lap. "Great."

"I mean, here's the thing: from a technical standpoint, it doesn't really make sense. So instead I've been thinking in terms of *why*. Why would everybody disappear? Without notice. Without warning. If it had been premeditated or, like, if everyone had decided to evacuate or something, there'd be a sign or a notice. They don't make decisions like that in a weekend, and if they did, surely Brad's or Tim's parents would have called or texted to let us know. We didn't hear anything about a planned evacuation. And even if they all had to leave in a hurry, that would have been obvious. But as you can see, the place does not look evacuated so much as . . . well, I don't know what."

"Like they vanished," Jason said.

Archer nodded. "Yeah," he said softly.

"But how?" Jason asked.

"I don't know. But that ties into this electrical conundrum. An event perpetrated upon the island caused both mysteries. But the how of the electricity is a tough nut, as well. Someone, or some *ones*, could have neutralized the power plant or cut off the electricity coming to the island, but that doesn't explain battery and motor dysfunction. Failure this complete is really a much larger-scale event."

"What could do it?"

"Man-made? A nuclear blast, maybe. A gigantic electromagnetic pulse. There are supposedly machines that can create an electromagnetic pulse capable of simulating a nuclear effect on electrical systems without all the death and damage, but you can't just pick one up at your local dollar store."

Jason practically whispered, "Maybe that's what happened."

"What? A nuclear blast? I doubt it. We would have felt it or seen it. And everything's still standing. It might explain the obliteration of everybody in town, but not why everything else looks like it always did."

"Yeah. Well, is there anything else that compares?"

"I suppose, theoretically, a powerful enough lightning storm or major geologic event could create enough electromagnetic force. I'm talking a storm or a tectonic shift of cataclysmic proportions, though. If either occurred, we were too close not to have felt it. A lightning storm that big or an earthquake? We would have sensed it. That's end-of-days-type stuff."

Tim sniffed. "The rapture."

Bradley said, "Dude, will you quit it with the rapture?"

Archer didn't miss a beat, as if he'd already considered the possibility: "The rapture might make sense from a religious point of view," he said, "but I doubt that's what happened here. If the popular theory that God would take only 'born-again Christians' is accurate, the town should have plenty of people left over. We have a good town, but the majority of people are not Christian by any stretch. I would expect a rapture to have actually left more people than it took. Unless they've got the rapture wrong, and God just takes everybody."

"Maybe God did take everybody," Tim said.

"Everybody but us?"

"I already told him all that," said Bradley. "It wasn't a rapture. But I think we're sort of ignoring the obvious here."

"What's that?" Archer asked, obviously intrigued.

"The creepy guy on the ferry? The complete disappearance of everyone? There's something spooky about all this, man. It's like a ghost movie or something."

"Oh." Archer was clearly disappointed. "I think we'll have more luck thinking through a rational explanation to a very real problem here. In the category of the supernatural, there are just too many possibilities and, therefore, room for too much irrational speculation."

"Dude, can't you talk like a normal person for once?" Bradley said.

Before Archer could answer, it was Jason's turn to break. "Why are you all being so calm about this?" He looked on the verge of tears.

Archer frowned. "Does getting upset help anything?"

"I don't know!"

There was silence.

Jason burned. "We might never see our families again."

Tim sniffed.

"Great," Bradley said. "Tim's crying again. Way to go, Jase."

Jason sat on his hands. "This is messed up, man. This is messed up."

Archer said, "We'll figure it out, Jason."

"Shut up!"

Archer winced. Finding no help from Bradley, he lifted the notebook to his face. But it was too dark to see the gibberish.

Night invaded the house. Their faces shimmered yellow and swam in shadows. Rain began to pelt the windows, then grew into a steady roar.

After a long silence, Bradley rose. "Forget this, man. You guys can sit around. I'm going back."

Tim looked up, frightened. "Back where?"

"To the mainland, what do you think?"

Bradley had spoken to Tim, but Jason looked up from the couch like a chastened child. Meekly, he reminded Bradley, "The boats don't work."

"I'll sail it. Kayak, I mean."

Archer stood. "Bradley, it's storming."

"Duh. But I'm not sitting around here all night."

He turned to leave. Tim followed him with his head, his tears surging again. Jason stared straight ahead, dumbfounded. Archer followed Bradley to the door. "It's too dangerous, man."

"Hey, here's something for you to calculate." Bradley opened the door. A mist swirled in around him. "If I paddle from here to the mainland to get help, what time will I get back?"

"Well—" Archer began.

"Dude! I'm just joking. You crack me up, Archway."

He punched Archer on the arm and turned to step out onto the stoop. Lightning flashed nearby.

Archer flinched.

"This is gonna be wild!" Bradley shouted in crazy exultation as he walked across the yard and disappeared into the watery veil. Thunder rocked the house, and Archer shut the door.

Tim called, "You just let him go?"

"Yeah."

"What if he disappears too?"

Archer cocked his head at Tim. "Are *you* going to try to stop him while he's in this state?"

Jason wanted to get a drink from the kitchen. He rose to leave and said, "You think he'll really try it?"

"I don't know," Archer said. "He's kind of unhinged at the moment, so maybe."

"Yes," said Tim. "He'll really try it."

If not for the lightning, Bradley might never have reached the ferry landing. The thick rain and the black night, previously decorated by Echo Island's many streetlights, had him pedaling blind. But the prolonged flashes of lightning lit his way.

Bradley dropped the bike on the gravel parking lot and headed straight for the machine room and the kayak. The lightning did not help in the building; in darkness and under the disorienting roar of the rain on the tin roof, he stumbled about, arms before him, feeling around like the newly blind. He felt along the wall to the right of the door, knocking random articles off tables and shelves in an attempt to stay clear of the boat ramps. He was already drenched from the rain, but falling into oily water was something else entirely.

Eventually, Bradley felt the hard shell of the kayak hanging on the wall just shy of the corner of the building. He lifted and pulled, and when he had it free, he could hear the rattle of articles inside: a paddle and a life jacket.

"Score." He suddenly felt a burst of energy.

Pulling the vessel down the rough grade adjacent to the ferry dock and entering the water, he squeezed into the rubber-sealed seat without hesitation and pushed off into the rocking channel between the island and the mainland.

The Pacific waters churned cold and dark, and the rain continued to fall unabated. The lightning frightened him now, despite its continued help. Without it, he could keep an approximate sense of bearing—the island was behind him. But with it, and bobbing in the wide-open sea without cover or comfort, he feared a fatal zap. The real danger lay at the fulcrum point of the island's disappearance from the rear horizon; in that brief limbo of nothing but ocean, in the space where neither shore could be seen, it would be easy to lose his bearings.

Bradley paddled harder against the water he couldn't see and against a fierce wind that seemed to have started only to oppose him. The roar of the rain on the ocean muffled even the thunder. Through the haze of rain in his eyes, the lightning-lit way seemed surrounded by waterfalls, like he was rounding the curve of the earth or reaching the end of the world.

Bradley realized he'd been paddling for too long for the lights of the mainland park not to be in view. Maybe he'd changed directions without realizing it. He'd only sailed the channel once at night, and the conditions were clear and calm then.

Bradley wondered if he'd diverted north or south.

Then he had a disturbing thought. If the electricity on the mainland was out too, there wouldn't be any lights to see. He hadn't felt like he'd turned. But it's hard to know *straight* in such conditions. If only he'd had the night sky or some other landmark. Or a compass.

Or some sense.

He yelled into the sky, a deep eruption from the gut.

Bradley thrived on control, on forcing his will onto any- thing and everything he pleased. The feeling of helplessness now was overwhelming, and he felt like he might explode into a million pieces. He seethed and pounded the kayak with his fist.

Tilting his face up to the black sky, he felt the rain fall heavy on his lips and closed eyelids.

Finally, he hung his head. Laying the paddle across his covered lap, he bobbed on the waves and tried to calm down.

After a few minutes, lightning flashed, and Bradley could see the faint outline of solid land thin and low on the horizon.

A thrill overtook him. "Ah!" he shouted in triumph. The paddle broke the water with gusto.

He cursed when he got close enough to realize he'd done a one-eighty and was heading back to the island. But he didn't stop, deciding this time to search the machine shop boats for a compass.

Every time Bradley found something that felt like a compass, he rushed outside to wait for the lightning's confirmation only to discover he was holding something else: a key ring, a sealed pack of chewing tobacco, a set of retractable headphones, an empty box of mints, and various round tools and electronics he couldn't identify.

After an hour and a half, Bradley finally felt a round, knobby protrusion near the wheel of one of the boats. This was odd because most boats now had electronic directional devices installed, but it was worth a try. The object felt like plastic, and although it was attached, he had no trouble snapping it off the dashboard. Bradley was not just strong, but frustrated.

In the sporadic light of the storm, he saw that he had at last liberated a compass. It was a spinning globe in a clear plastic shell, and after grabbing a screwdriver and screws from a table he'd found in his previous search, he screwed the base onto the kayak's bow.

His purpose revived and his energy renewed, Bradley set out again.

Jason had no idea what time it was, but the house still shuddered in the storm. He'd woken from a restless sleep to get a drink of water, even though he wasn't really thirsty, and discovered for the first time that the wall clock in the kitchen had stopped at 8:56, a minute off the time the clock at Archer's house read. Just shy of 9:00 a.m. His parents would have been in their Sunday school class. His brother would have been in the church's back lot with his buddies, taking turns watching each other trying to injure themselves on skateboards.

Eight fifty-something.

Jason didn't want to think something catastrophic had happened, but if it had, he hoped it had been painless. He briefly pictured his family disintegrating in a bright flash, but shook his head, hurling the thought away.

In the living room, Tim was sprawled out on the sofa. Archer was sitting upright in Jason's father's recliner, the green notebook clutched to his chest like a teddy bear. Their eyes were closed, but none of them could sleep.

The bottled water was lukewarm to the touch. Jason eyed the sink and wondered if the town's water system relied at all on electricity. Would the water eventually give out or turn bad? He was tired, but his overactive imagination easily conjured up images of an island overrun by sewage, of having to boil pond water over open fires, and of the four of them living like castaways on a postapocalyptic island, living out some *Lord of the Flies* nightmare.

Leaning against the kitchen counter in the dark, he'd almost drifted to sleep, trying hard to inspire a dream about all this being a dream, when a loud banging made him jump.

The bottle fell and water poured out onto the tile.

"Is someone knocking?" he heard Tim say.

Jason felt his way back into the living room.

Lightning flashed, highlighting Tim's deer-in-headlights expression.

"Shh," Jason said.

Archer stirred, yawned.

"Shh!" Jason hissed.

"What?"

Six loud bangs on the door.

All three turned.

"Careful," Jason said, as Archer rose, stretched, and walked to the entryway.

"It's probably Bradley," he said.

"Maybe he found help back on the mainland," Tim said. "What time is it?"

Archer shuffled closer.

"Careful, man," Jason repeated. "There are others out there."

The visitor pounded on the door again, rattling the glass.

"Open up, you buttheads!"

"Bradley," Jason said, relieved.

Archer turned the dead bolt and had barely cracked the door when Bradley pushed in, dripping water everywhere.

Bradley looked at him, undecided whether to jab with a retort or with a closed fist. Before he could respond, Tim said, "Did you make it? Did you find someone?"

Bradley looked at him with a profound distress. He sputtered, "It's not there."

"What?" said Archer. "What's not there?"

"The park. The mainland."

"What about it?"

"It's gone."

6

GHOSTS

What do you mean, it's gone?" Jason asked.

"It's gone! The whole thing. It's just . . . not there," Bradley shouted.

"There's no way—" Tim started.

"Tim, it's gone!"

"Maybe you got turned around," Archer said.

"Not a chance," Bradley insisted.

"How could you see out there anyway? We can try again in the morning, in the daylight."

"Try if you want, man. I'm telling you, it's not there. I had a compass. I stayed east, I'm positive. I paddled for at least an hour after I couldn't see the island behind me anymore. It's just not there."

Archer closed the door. "Look, Bradley, you're tired and wet. And frustrated. It would have been really easy to get turned around in the storm."

"Dude, I've been sailing these waters my whole life. I don't get turned around." His one-eighty notwithstanding. "And I had a compass!"

"The whole coast of Washington State did not just disappear."

When lightning struck, Archer noted the downcast look on Bradley's face again.

The house went dark. Bradley said, "The whole population of our town disappeared. I don't know, man. I knew where I was going. I found the island again going due west on the compass. But due east, there's nothing there."

Archer dared not press the matter.

Jason lit some candles, and a gloom settled on all of them and then, a weariness.

Weariest of all was Bradley; he sloshed from the entryway to the couch and collapsed, wet clothes and all, next to Tim. With the others watching in terrified silence, he closed his eyes.

Tim looked to Archer as if for help.

Archer whispered to Jason, "We'll check it out tomorrow."

They all sought sleep then, despite the waning darkness and the continuing din of the storm, but sleep still eluded them. Three hours later, shortly after dawn, the storm had passed, but the entire island lay shrouded in fog. Thick white mist crowded every way, like a swirling, slowly encroaching army of ghosts.

They couldn't even see the street from the Georges' front door.

Bradley had helped himself to some of Jason's brother's clothes. It irritated Jason. Either one of the others would have asked first. And Bradley in Scott's khaki cargo shorts and blue Nike tank top just made Scott's disappearance, *the whole family's disappearance*, that much more unsettling.

"When the fog clears," Archer said, "maybe we can sail out for the park again."

"Who's this *we*?" Bradley said. "You've never sailed in your life."

"Okay. *You guys* can go out again."

"Not me," said Bradley. "Already did it. Maybe you thought I was dreaming or hallucinating, but—"

"Actually, I was thinking you got lost in the storm."

"I didn't. And that's the last time I'm going to tell you." The look on Bradley's face said he meant it. "I don't know how it happened—far as I'm concerned, that's for you to figure out—but it's not there. Understand? End of story. Not there. If one of you guys wants to go looking for the mainland, have at it. But I'm not going out there again. Something crazy's going on, and I'm not gonna paddle out there just to turn around and find out that Echo Island's disappeared too. Then what're you gonna do? You can try your own luck if you want. But leave me out."

"Fair enough," Archer said. He and Jason exchanged looks. "But," Archer continued, "I still think, however weird this is, there's a logical explanation."

"If you say I got lost in the storm again, I swear I will feed you your own kneecaps."

Archer, unperturbed, said, "Well, I'm going to ride out to the power station. Maybe I can figure out how to get some electricity going again. If we get some power restored, we'll be able to check the TV or the radio or get some kind of communication device working. I'm under the assumption now that the island is indeed empty."

"Pots don't fall off carts by themselves," Tim said.

"Fine, *mostly* empty," said Archer. "In which case, our best hope is seeing if we can find any news about the island, or contact the outside world."

Apropos of nothing, Tim said, "I wonder if the Mariners won yesterday."

Bradley punched him on the arm.

Archer rolled his eyes. "Okay if I borrow a backpack?" he asked Jason.

Jason grabbed one from his closet. Archer put the green notebook and two bottled waters in it, slung it over his shoulder, and started for the door.

"You don't want one of us to come with?" Jason asked.

"I'll be fine." Archer didn't want anybody getting in his way. "It's not that far, and with any luck, I'll get some juice flowing in this dead burg."

"You don't believe in luck."

"Well, I believe in it more than I do some other things."

Jason faked a smile and watched Archer disappear on his bike into the milky veil.

"He's so strange," Bradley suddenly said. "Him and his logical explanations. It doesn't take Encyclopedia Brown to figure out what's going on here isn't natural."

Neither Tim nor Jason bothered responding, partly out of wariness of challenging their irascible friend, and partly out of the inclination to agree with him.

"Dudes, we should totally go check out the woods behind the Bee Market," Bradley suggested. "Maybe there's clues. Maybe that person is hiding out in there."

Jason and Tim sat at the round table in the George family's breakfast nook, pondering the ghostly gauze swimming in the backyard.

"If that person wanted to be found, I think we would've found them, right?" Jason said. "I mean, at this point, it just seems like poking around is looking for trouble."

"What're we gonna do, just sit around all day?" Bradley asked.

"We have to wait for Archer. If we leave and he comes back, he won't know where we are."

"A note. Ever hear of it? I think pens still work."

"For all we know he'll run into trouble out there," said Tim. "We should stay in case he comes back for help."

"Nah. If I know Archway, he's already there fiddling with circuits and whatnot. He'll be fine, man. He's probably already forgotten about us. Come on."

Tim looked at Jason, in want of a reasonable rebuttal.

Jason was irritated. "Go with him if you want."

"Sweet," Bradley said. "Let's go, Timmy."

Tim obeyed, trailing Bradley, who was practically bouncing to the door.

"I hope you both get lost in the woods," Jason called out after them.

Cocking his head slightly sideways, Bradley pretended to waft passed gas from his hindquarters as he walked away. He called out to Jason, "Have lunch on the table when we get home, sweetie."

The door slammed and they were gone.

The mist in Jason's backyard cloaked the fence. It didn't seem to be dissipating at all. He reckoned it was nearly nine o'clock—it felt like nine o'clock anyway, if feelings were to be trusted—yet the whiteness held, diffused, the glow of dawn.

The silence was unnerving.

A note under a magnet curled out from the refrigerator. Jason reached for the sunflower-adorned stationery and was greeted by his mother's perfect cursive.

John, forget to water the plants.

It was a note to his dad dating back almost two weeks.

The wording was intentional, part of a family inside joke. His mother once quipped that his father always ignored whatever instructions she left, so she was going to start instructing the opposite of what she wanted. Ever since, notes graced the fridge reading *Leave the wobbly table leg alone* and *Don't transplant the flowers*. Once she even posted a "honey do" list with items like *Lie around on the couch, Let the trash pile up*, and *Ignore the broken garage door*. All the men in Jason's family found his mom's jokey passive aggression quite charming, but they all continued to ignore the notes (or the purpose of the notes) anyway.

Jason crumpled up the note to discard it, but without realizing it, put the wad in his pocket. He climbed the stairs, paused at the landing as if deciding which direction to turn, and went left toward his parents' room.

The four-poster bed lay before him, a sight once pleasing in its homey appeal and promise of comfort, but now disturbing in its conspicuous unkemptness. The comforter had been pulled back, exposing a swirl of recently used sheets. His mother never left the house without making the bed.

In the empty bathroom, the sunlight through the open window set dull glows in the glass row of his mother's perfumes and cosmetic potions.

The silence here was almost too much.

Jason exited and crossed the landing toward his bedroom, stopping at his brother's.

The first thing to hit him was the first thing that always hit him when entering Scott's room—the odor. Absolutely unique to these four walls, it was a pungent concoction of fungal feet and hamster cage. He noted that Scott's hamster, Payton, had indeed vanished. What hadn't vanished was the smell his mother had sought vainly to overcome. They eventually counted their blessings that the malodorous funk lived in Scott's room and Scott's room only.

The red bedspread and navy sheets intertwined like a licorice twist and labeled the always-unmade bed with a question mark.

Jason sat on the left edge of the mattress and surveyed the soccer and lacrosse trophies on the bureau. Posters surrounded the space—team photos of the Seattle Seahawks and the Seattle Supersonics, a shot of Seahawk great Steve Largent receiving a pass, David Beckham "bending it," legend Pelé doing the same, and clichéd portraits of Switchfoot, Green Day, Linkin Park, and P.O.D. They were images of people frozen, windows into a real life that had been interrupted, an outside world that may or may not have existed anymore. Once Scott's mementos, they now seemed to Jason like mementos of Scott.

There were too many angles, too many pieces to put together. Like Archer, Jason wanted to figure it all out before despairing of what happened. But the puzzle seemed too large and kept growing larger. It looked bigger than him, bigger than all four of them.

Jason missed his family, so now that his friends were gone and he was all alone, he went in his own room, locked the door, and cried.

Archer knew nothing about power stations, but he quickly deduced the fenced-in site didn't actually generate electricity. Ten dulled silver transformers adjoined a little red brick building down a rocky slope on the island's northern coast. After he'd snapped the lock on the outer gate with bolt cutters pilfered from the Vawter family's garage, he read the gray stenciled lettering on the green door: WWEC SUBSTATION 204.

Archer had to kick the door in, which was a feat in itself given his scrawny legs. Once inside, he found the darkness frustrating. The murkiness outside shrouded the room from daylight. In the dim haze and with feeling hands, he could tell that the walls were hung with broad metal boxes. He figured they held fuses and circuit breakers. He expected a large control panel and a desk layout with chairs and monitors. There may have been a manual of some sort in there, but he'd need more light to find it. It bugged him immensely that to understand the thing, he needed the help of the thing itself.

Back in the yard he wandered among the transformers, imagining what it might feel like with the current active. He imagined his skin tingling, every hair on his body standing at attention. In the lingering fog, the towers were an eerie monument to industrialization, a sleek steel Stonehenge memorializing a silence and a stillness they used to eradicate.

Archer was a fan of lines, of connections and congruencies, of right angles, of symmetry. Despite the chaotic décor of his home, he desired patterns, discernible trajectories, textures with referents. As with all things, he viewed art with a mathematic straightforwardness. He loved the idea of a system, which is why he felt comfortable in the company of the transformers.

Despite knowing full well no current flowed, he hesitated to touch them.

Though he couldn't see even ten feet in any direction, Archer could hear the whisper of the waves brushing the stones at the bottom of the grade outside the yard. Unless Echo Island hosted another power station he'd never seen, the power came from the mainland, no doubt in huge cables under the ocean running through the ground beneath his feet. If restoring the power was possible, Archer trusted the responsible authorities would see to it. He wasn't keen on rowing out to the mainland that Bradley said didn't exist anymore.

Not there. As if such a thing were possible.

He found it impossible to follow the wires. He couldn't see them. He'd been walking in fifteen feet of visibility for going on forty-five minutes, with only the occasional hint of cable above him—high, high above him—and not only did he not think he'd find a real power plant, he didn't think he could find his way back.

Archer had journeyed across countless streets but never saw street signs. He followed electric poles until they led up grassy slopes or into other places that he didn't feel like navigating the bike through. Occasionally, he'd board a sidewalk and register his location by the sign on a door or window, but he'd long since wandered into undeveloped wooded areas. They were parks maybe, or just the acres and acres of Pacific Northwest forest, miles and miles of Echo Island scenic routes.

Something occurred to him while on this trek, albeit briefly. *If* a sudden, say, rapture-like event had vanished everyone, why didn't anything on the island seem interrupted? Sure, traffic would be sparse on a Sunday morning, but the sudden and surprise interruption of life might have left a crashed car here and there. There'd be litter in the streets, food left out on tables uneaten. Even if the event had caused no structural or environmental damage, it would have at least left signs of life interrupted. The island looked the same as it always had, but the actual signs of *life*, of activity, were gone with the inhabitants. It was like a stage set for a play that hadn't begun.

It was a reset, he thought.

But the thought didn't fit, not yet, so he filed it away and instead tried to figure out where he was walking.

Bradley changed his mind when he and Tim got to the Bee Market.

"I'm gonna walk down to the liquor store," he said.

"Why? It's not open."

"Everything's open, dude."

Tim puckered, then frowned. "That's stealing."

"I'll keep a log, how 'bout that? With all my purchases. So, when Jesus comes back with everybody after the Tribulation, I can pay the liquor store guy what I owe."

"That's not funny."

Tim stuck his hand in the gap between the market's once-electric doors and pried them open. He said, "I'm not going to look around in those woods by myself."

"I don't blame you. Come with, if you want then."

Tim pushed the right door back on its track.

Bradley said, "Or hang out in the market. I'll meet you over there later."

Tim walked into the shadowy Bee Market, leaving Bradley there smirking like a fool, oblivious to the fog engulfing him.

Inside the Bee Market, the faint whiff of rot tickled Tim's nostrils. Meat had begun to spoil, dairy to sour. The lack of refrigeration and irrigation left an earthy reek hanging over the produce section.

He first located matches near the picnic items, then lit all six kerosene lanterns found in the small housewares section and scattered them strategically at six equidistant points around the store. The light was sparse.

Tim took one up and wandered the aisles slowly, unnerved by the sound of his own breathing. Maybe he'd made a mistake going in alone. The store was awfully dark.

A shuffled footstep squealed on the tile, and he gave himself goosebumps.

Rounding the corner of the breakfast aisle, he came to the meat cases on the back wall, where the odor lingered strongly and the swinging butcher's door stood waiting.

That's where the other person had been. Maybe he still wasn't alone.

It took him five minutes to muster the will to push the door open. His hand shook, shining a jittery beam into the dark room. Heart pounding, Tim crept through the room, past the break room and office, and into the pitch-black storage room. It stunk of turning meat.

The exit door lay ahead, and by his feet (but out of his view) lay the fallen pot, the pot of the clang that had originally alerted Bradley and him to another presence.

His next step sent it skittering across the floor. The clanging was unnerving. Tim winced.

When the pot finally rattled to a stop, the only thing louder in his head than the metallic echo of its course was his heartbeat. He stifled imminent hyperventilation.

The wall of clouds outside the back door did not appeal to him at all. He reentered the store and walked the aisles again, looking at boxes and bags like someone tours art in a museum.

Tim wasn't hungry, but food—packaged food—appealed to his psychological and emotional appetites. He lost track of time staring passively at rows of geometric rainbows—boxes and cartons forming bright pixels in a Technicolor display. Here was where Tim was most comfortable. Here was where Tim would have stayed forever if he could have.

Before smashing the glass on the door to the liquor store, Bradley tried the handle and found it unlocked.

Callisto Liquors was painted hunter green and had brass trim and windows that were either tinted or very dusty. The store centered a five-store strip mall collectively dubbed The Shops at Echo Point. While each storefront maintained a unique look, they were all connected by a common utility hall in the rear. The architecture revealed a vague attempt at a scene of Dickensian charm: the chocolatier and the stationery store both spelled shop "shoppe," and there was a Tea Pantry and a used bookstore called Pickwick's Paperbacks.

Inside Callisto Liquors, Bradley surveyed all the bottles. So many options and nobody to card him. The mystery of the missing adults had this intriguing upside. Something inside him trembled at the notion of lifted limitations. He could quite possibly do whatever he wanted now.

It bothered him that he'd probably have to drink alone. Or with Tim, who wasn't that much fun. He had taken a bottle from his father's stash on the camping trip, but none of the other guys wanted to partake. Maybe now that they weren't in danger of getting in trouble with anybody, he could convince them to let loose. But then, it bothered him that they weren't really in danger of getting in trouble either. What's the point if there's no one to watch? No one to catch you?

The cedars and sycamores gave way to steel-beamed giants, and Archer was happy to see he'd been following the wires even though he couldn't see them through the fog. He still held out hope that he could make sense of the thing at their convergence.

He strode among the tall legs of the stickmen who held up the island's electric current on their cloud-shrouded shoulders. After an hour of walking tower to tower, having left streets behind, he had no idea what part of the island he was on. Electric line towers weren't things he normally thought to look for; they were always in the background.

The grass flicked dew onto his bare ankles. Down a slope, Archer journeyed into a wide bowl in the earth from which the fog seemed to lift. To his left he could see the white line of a curb, and he diverted from his previous trajectory along the electric towers to investigate.

The curb bordered a parking lot, and Archer walked up the asphalt incline to discover the Echo Island Historical Center, a small museum of island artifacts, legends, and lore that doubled as a tourist information center. Outside the heavy black door stood a statue of a bearded man in turn-of-the-century seaman's garb, mist clinging to his arms and torso like white streamers. He held a lantern in his left hand and a set of keys in his right. A silver plate on the pedestal read: VIRGIL GROSSET, FOUNDER OF ECHO ISLAND, 1895.

Archer had visited the center only once on a fourth-grade field trip. He hadn't thought of the place in ages, but he vividly recalled a young Bradley Hershon performing chin-ups on Virgil Grosset's stone arms. He also remembered looking at the framed, yellowed maps on the wall with Jason.

The door was unlocked.

The view outside Jason's bedroom window was stark white. His pillow lay damp with tears under his cheek. Raising his stiff body from the bed, he shuffled to the door.

On the landing he called, "Hello?"

Downstairs he saw that his friends were still gone.

In the kitchen he stared at the food in the pantry but didn't feel hungry enough to eat anything. The faint smell of food turning in the dead fridge made him queasy.

He leaned against the counter by the sink. The clock was still stuck at 8:56.

He shoved his hands in his pockets. His left fist touched something, and he removed the crumpled note from his mother to his father. He flattened it out between his palms, running it over the edge of the counter to iron out the wrinkles. He put it back under its magnet on the refrigerator door.

Jason's solitude suddenly felt like vulnerability. He didn't like that feeling, so he decided to pedal out to the Bee Market to look for Tim and Bradley.

Halfway down Royal Garden, he hopped off his bike to walk instead. The fog was so dense it just didn't feel safe speeding along.

Just outside the big brick Royal Garden subdivision sign, he cut right across the soccer field bordering the church, assuming he was saving time and energy. The wet grass itched his legs. One hundred yards later, he realized he should have followed the ditch he encountered left instead of right. The gravestone was the first indication.

He'd wound up around the far side of the church, between the rear parking lot and the woods that circled Cutter Pond like a garland. He'd wandered into the church's old cemetery.

They didn't bury bodies there anymore; the most recent burial had been in 1968. Ever since, the church had interred its departed with the rest of Echo Island's dead in the cemetery that, since the late 1950s, had begun inching its way into the windswept ocean vista of Minuai Fields on the island's west coast.

Lost in an old graveyard in a disorienting fog. Creepy.

Jason stopped and tried to regain his bearings. The stuff was so thick, he couldn't tell which way lay the church and which, the pond. He figured that the grave inscriptions faced the church, so he walked that way. The world was silent, but not quite. His steps squished on the wet grass, but there was something else.

Someone else?

He stopped, and the other sound—footsteps?—continued.

He couldn't discern the origin.

He turned around and around, careful not to make another sound.

His blood ran cold.

He craned his neck, wincing in anticipation of what terrible thing he might see. In the fog over his right shoulder, about ten feet away, a vein of mist appeared to shimmy snakelike into its own opacity. It was just a wisp, but it was distinct.

He swallowed, put his hands up as if to defend himself and followed it slowly, searching for that movement.

It stayed just barely out of sight. In the near distance, enshrouded in a more stationary haze, it was like a strip of fog had become a swirl of ribbon.

Then it vanished.

Jason stopped.

He listened.

He heard nothing.

His arms tingled with gooseflesh. The hair on his neck stood up. He was just about to sprint into the billows when a young woman in a flowing white dress suddenly passed before him and disappeared.

7

GHOST TOWN

Bradley loaded a heavy sack of liquor bottles into a backpack he'd found in the stock room. Tim, who had finally left the Bee Market to rejoin his friend, stood there dumbly, staring at him.

"What?" Bradley said, annoyed.

"Do you really think you should be doing this?"

"Look, Baby Huey, this may be the end of the world. I intend to have one last party."

He went behind the counter and began rifling through the shelves beneath.

"What are you doing?" Tim said.

"Looking for a corkscrew."

Bradley stopped, staring at the space within the counter. His face looked blank.

"What's wrong?" asked Tim.

"You know," Bradley said. "I bet they had a gun back here."

"Why do you say that?"

"I don't know. It just reminds me of where, like, convenience stores keep their guns."

"I doubt they had a gun. There's not crime like that on the island."

Bradley sighed, thinking. "You know, the police station's not far from here. Just a ways up the road. We never checked it."

"Bradley, if you're saying you want to find a gun, I think it's a bad idea."

"Dude, we are not alone out here, and if whoever we heard kidnapped everybody else, we're going to need protection, don't you think?"

"First you want to get hammered. Then you want to get armed. Sounds brilliant."

Bradley did not like when Tim pushed back. "Maybe you should mind your own business," he said.

"Well, I'm not walking to the police station. Let's go back to Jason's."

"Dude, you're killing me!"

It never took much to convince Tim that what Bradley wanted was more important than what he did. So Tim sighed, which Bradley interpreted as compliance.

They walked uphill into the fog, Tim lagging behind in a steady rhythm of huffs and puffs. Bradley increased his pace.

The Echo Island City Police Headquarters building was not large. A lobby, a set of office cubicles, a locker room, an evidence room and armory, and a five-cell jail all occupied about two thousand square feet of space. They were tight quarters, to be sure, but Tim was right about the island's near nonexistent crime element—public intoxication and teenage vandalism were the most common offenses. So the station did not frequently require full capacity of either offices or inmates.

The place looked oddly clean and organized. It did not look as if anyone had left in a hurry. Desks were clear and orderly, chairs pushed in and straightened. There were no half-empty coffee cups laying about, no errant pens or paperwork. The tile floors looked recently waxed. A decrepit dot matrix printer dangled exactly one perforated section of paper neatly from its spindles, a squat white tongue mocking them.

The two steel doors leading to the jail were open, as were the cell doors.

"Hey, go in there for a second," Bradley joked.

"Uh-huh. And then you wouldn't be able to find the key."

"You could just eat your way out, all Cookie Monster and whatnot."

Tim shot him a look, like *very funny*.

"Oh, hey," said Bradley, "Keys are right there." A wide silver loop holding five fat keys hung on a hook right inside the second entry door.

Tim started to leave. "Let's go, man."

Bradley followed him back into the station house but said, "Hold up a minute."

He crossed the labyrinth of open offices in the main room, stopping once to lift a heavy, black belt off a table to see its holster held no firearm. He then passed through a door marked in white stenciled letters, EVIDENCE / ARMORY / MAINTENANCE.

Tim waited and watched, and eventually Bradley returned, obviously distraught.

"What's up?" Tim said.

"This door's been busted open. And there aren't any guns in there. None. Not even a TASER. No ammo. Nothing."

"Um . . ."

"Why would they be gone, man? Who would take all the guns?"

Tim couldn't tell if Bradley was scared or just disappointed that he didn't get to pack any heat. "I think we should head back."

"Yeah," Bradley said, definitely more concerned now than disappointed. "Yeah, okay."

Jason was sure it was a girl and not a ghost. Or maybe a ghost-girl. But it wasn't a trick of the fog. He entertained that theory for only a second. No. He had clearly seen a girl in a white dress pass in front of him.

"Hello," he said quietly, too quietly, almost as if he didn't want her to hear.

He couldn't hear her footsteps anymore and now he said it louder: "Hello." Firm, stern, making sure to sound like a man who could fight a ghost if he needed to. Just a little bit louder, he said, "I saw you."

He stopped to listen, halfway hoping she'd feel guilty for ignoring him and return, sorry for freaking him out. His eyes searched the mist, darting back and forth over every shadowy crease and swirl. He threw some more words out: "I won't hurt you."

For some reason, although he wasn't being quiet anymore, he didn't want to yell.

Maybe this girl was the one who lived in the cabin. Maybe she knew how to make sense of the gibberish notebooks. Maybe she witnessed what happened to everybody.

Jason listened for another few seconds, staggering around in a furtive three-sixty, and finally began walking forward. He had no sense of his bearings. He wasn't even sure if he was going in the direction she'd passed, but he kept pressing forward into the cloudy murk in front of him. A face suddenly appeared, and he nearly jumped out of his skin until he realized it was his own pale reflection in the glass of the church window. He had almost walked into the side of the white clapboard building.

And just like that, when the mist seemed the most hopelessly thick, the fog began to dissipate. He wondered if it had rolled in with the girl, a strange ethereal procession summoned by her presence, and it had rolled off now to follow her wherever she had gone.

He turned away from the church toward the cemetery behind him and watched the mist slither away with time-lapse effect, the smoky white tendrils sliding against the narrow tombstones.

The girl had not gone in the direction of town, he was sure of it. So he abandoned his plan to reach the Bee Market and retraced his steps back to the parking lot. He looked at the looming tree line of the woods. The fog was still settled in there, probably churning off the warming water of Cutter Pond in the middle.

He plodded forward.

In the Echo Island Historical Center, Archer found a box of matches in the receptionist desk and began lighting every candle and oil lantern he could find. He glanced at the row of desktop computers lining the wall just inside the front door and pursed his lips. It would be so much easier if he could google this predicament.

Instead, he took one of the lanterns in his hand and began making his methodical rounds, doing his "Archway thing," as Bradley might have put it. The center maintained a small library, nothing extensive, just five long oak bookcases holding books mostly related to coastal and island history, reference books about seafaring, forestry, and gardening, and, of course, plenty of town records full of boring lists of meetings, minutes, and deliberations. He thought about adding to the last Echo Island record book, "Town vanishes. Game over. The end."

It was the artwork on the wall that triggered his attention. One framed print, in particular, caught his eye. It was not an especially old work. Under unreflective glass and bordered by a simple cherrywood frame, the scene was a ship in the middle of a storm, a big foamy wave about to push against a scattering of rocks rising out of the dark green sea. It was a night scene, the ship dark brown with streaks of gray, the sky brown and orange. The entire image looked as if it had been covered in a grayish filter. A silver plaque affixed to the frame was engraved in a simple font: CREUSA, THE GHOST SHIP 1889.

Something about that name—*Creusa*—rattled Archer's memory, some artifact prying free in the back of his mind. He couldn't place it. It wouldn't come out to identify itself. But he knew what to do next.

Among the selection of books chronicling the Pacific Northwest's coastal history, he found a volume titled *Spooky Tales of the Salty Seas*. It was a book written for children, really, something like the Time-Life books on Bigfoot and UFOs that were designed to spark kids' interest in local history. The short book cataloged its entries alphabetically, and Archer didn't even need to scan an index. There on page twelve was the entry titled "Creusa."

During a great storm in October 1889, the storied ship called the *Creusa*, named after a figure in Greek mythology, was caught in great throes of danger off the western coast of Washington, just north of its destination, the tiny outpost called Echo Island. The ship left port in Anchorage, Alaska, not many days prior; the journey was intended to be a short and, no doubt, safe one. In the cold morning light, fishermen spotted the ship stuck in the rocks of Echo Island's northern harbor, listing helplessly, its torn sail flapping in the breeze. The storm was gone. And so were the *Creusa*'s twenty-four boarders. From the captain down to the lowliest shipmate, not a soul was found.

Did they abandon ship? Were they swept overboard? Were they kidnapped by pirates?

Or was it something more sinister?

To add more strangeness to the mystery, the captain's logbook contained just one entry, which ended abruptly, midsentence, as if he had been crudely—and permanently—interrupted.

The remains of the *Creusa* were dismantled and repurposed or destroyed. Her passengers were never accounted for, and what fell upon them remains a mystery. But to this day, fishermen far into the sea off the safe shores of Echo Island say they can sometimes hear the low moans of their ghosts rolling along with the steady waves. They are looking for their ship. They are looking for home.

Archer stared at the dramatic illustration of the *Creusa* that accompanied the entry. It looked somewhat like the painting hanging on the wall, but the book's artist had thought to include a small skeletal hand holding up a lantern in the boat's wave-crashed stern.

It was a children's book. He should have expected it would not provide any key insights into either the *Creusa*'s real fate, or their own. But something inside him seemed to warm, as if he had actually gotten closer to the solution to the mystery.

He closed the book and rose to reexamine the painting. What bothered him most about the entire scene was how wild it was. Archer was most comfortable indoors, looking at books, crunching numbers, tracing lines, making predictions, and charting trajectories based on available data and experience. A ship in a storm was the very opposite of all predictability. You can chart your course by map or stars, as he was sure the *Creusa*'s captain had done. But the sea is chaos, the skies unmasterable. They are each too vast, too full of possibilities.

Archer thought for a second what it might be like to be on that ship, to feel that you may at any second be wrecked, submerged, overthrown. Archer always thought drowning might be the worst way to die. But he didn't know what he would have done if he felt a shipwreck was imminent.

How did all twenty-four passengers just . . . vanish? No trace. How could they have all been swept overboard and none of their bodies ever been found washed up on the shores of the island?

For Archer, the idea of some ghostly solution was out of the question. There had to be a rational explanation for their disappearance. And for the whole town's disappearance, in his situation. But at the moment, he felt like that ship in the picture, without control and totally at the mercy of the overwhelming vastness of the world.

He needed to sit down.

Returning to the table, he retrieved the green notebook once again. The rolling, lolling swirls of the scribbles on those pages now before his eyes were like the waves of that stormy sea—unknowable, not navigable, overwhelming in their continuous onslaught. Word after word—if they were even words at all—streaming along, line after line, page after page, holding in their hammering grasp, as far as he knew, the keys to everything. Archer stared at them, into them, through them. He hoped to walk on these waves, to tame them.

Bradley and Tim returned to Jason's house. Tim was disappointed to find that neither of their friends had returned, and especially so after Bradley immediately began pouring himself drinks.

"Are you sure that's a good idea?" Tim asked.

"Tim," said Bradley. "My main man. I'm not sure of anything right now."

Tim had never seen Bradley scared. Angry, yes. Frustrated, definitely. He'd seen him tired and even confused. But he didn't think he'd ever seen him scared.

"Here," Bradley said. He pushed a glass of brown liquor across the table. "Sit a spell, junior."

Tim looked down at the glass. He had been drinking with Bradley before. He never liked it. He didn't like the illegality of it. But he also didn't like the taste. And he especially didn't like what happened to Bradley when he drank. As far as Tim was concerned, Bradley was the last person on earth who needed to lower his inhibitions.

And while he hated saying no to him, Tim said it anyway. "No, I'm good."

"Well, I guess you are," Bradley said. "You. Jason. Archway. You're all so good. It makes me sick."

It sounded like drunk talk, but he hadn't yet taken a sip.

Tim walked away. He went to look out the large picture window in the living room. The fog was gone, but the expanse above the houses was milky white, as if one thick monstrous cloud had settled over the island. It made the sky look like a big blank page.

"Is there anything good in the pantry?" he called out.

Bradley didn't answer.

Tim hung his head. He didn't feel hungry, but that had never before stopped him from eating. He thought of all those beautiful cereal boxes back at the grocery.

"Since they're not here, I'm going for a walk," he called over his shoulder.

Bradley muttered from the kitchen, "Whatever."

Tim was scared to go outside alone, scared that whoever was in the Bee Market might surface again. But he walked out the door anyway. In that moment, anywhere felt safer than the house with a drunken, scared Bradley.

Without a goodbye, he headed in the direction of the Bee Market.

The fog eerily hovered just inside the woods around Cutter Pond. Jason was reluctant to reenter it, but he was sure the girl had gone in there. That is, if he hadn't hallucinated the whole thing.

Slowly he stepped, the softest crunch of grass and leaves beneath his feet sounding so much louder in his ears than they actually were. The mist indeed seemed draped along the trees, large swaths of thick vapor. It looked like it could even be *felt*, and he pushed his hand through, half expecting some material resistance.

Once inside the tree line, he could not see but three or four feet in any direction. Still he pressed on, slowly, gingerly. Tree after tree came into view. The air was still, silent. There was no rattling of squirrels on fallen leaves, no fluttering of birds in the branches, not so much as a frog's croak from the direction of the pond.

He put one foot in front of the other and made his way cautiously to the interior woods, knowing he couldn't be very far from the pond.

As he neared the shore, the ground began to slope, becoming grassier. His feet were practically in mud when he stopped. There was no wind, no ripple on the pond. It was smooth as glass and the fog hovered over it like a low storm over a sea.

Then he heard it.

In the normal din of the forest, he might not have heard the sound. But in the eerie quiet of the moment, it was unmistakable. A foot striking the ground, perhaps into a protruding root. A hollow *thump*.

He whirled around and saw nothing, of course, but the white veil around him. Still he called in the direction of the noise. "Who's there? Hello?"

Nothing.

"I know you're there. I saw you before. Please."

He tried to sound unthreatening.

He listened intently. The quiet was unnerving.

Again, less loudly. "Please."

Jason thought he could hear something now. What was it? A shuffling, like small feet through grass. Was it moving away? Or nearer?

It seemed to get quieter. Definitely moving away.

And right as he was about to run in the direction of the noise, thrusting himself into the obstacle course of a rush of unseen trees, a face pushed through the fog before him, and with it a long mane of brown hair. It was a girl in a white dress.

8

INTERSECTIONS

It finally occurred to Tim just how unnaturally quiet the island was. The complete hush of anything mechanical or electronic was spooky enough, but he listened for birds, for the rustling of a breeze, for *something*. There was nothing. After the whole world sounded like it was crashing into their town during the thunderstorm, it was like they'd all been shut into some sensory deprivation chamber. The place looked the same, but it didn't sound, smell, even *feel* the same.

And maybe it wasn't the same. Maybe they hadn't reached the island at all but some cruel facsimile, some holographic hoax set as a trap by . . . what?

He tried to think about what Archer might say. What if it wasn't that everyone vanished, but that they weren't on Echo Island at all? Archer had gone on and on once before about alternate dimensions, otherworlds created at some supposed cataclysmic cosmic moment, a parallel universe with higher elements and greater natural laws than our own. Archer never got far into that kind of thing before Tim got bored and tuned him out, or Bradley got bored and started making fun.

Tim now wished Bradley had come with him. He did not like being alone with his thoughts. And as the edifices of the town center came closer and closer, he did not like being alone with whomever—or whatever—might be out there.

Still, he walked down the sidewalk toward the Bee Market alone, creeping slowly with his left shoulder against the brick walls of the storefronts, pausing before every window and door to listen and peer in from a parallel angle, and then rushing past only to slow again when he reached the security of the exterior brick.

Slowly, slowly, slowly, Tim proceeded this way until he at last reached the grocery store again. Only then did it dawn on him that the dark interior of the store would be immensely more frightening than the daylight outside. And yet, he felt inexorably drawn in. The familiarity, the predictability, the orderliness of the place all offered a comfort he couldn't explain. He opened the door and entered.

At the historical society building, Archer felt like he was on a roll. Green notebook pressed flat on the table before him, he made his own scribbles on a sheet of paper next to it. He had convinced himself the writing was real. Not gibberish. A cypher. Some kind of code. Once his mind got going, it was difficult to turn off, and his points of inquiry and postulations began to divide into multiple streams of thought, branching off each other, intersecting and radiating out in bursting arrays of limbic impressions.

For one thing, he realized why the situation felt so familiar to him. The historical anecdote of the *Creusa* became a referent pointing him back further. The lost colony of Roanoke! Yes. This had happened before. An entire town had disappeared. When old compatriots had returned to the town, they found it completely abandoned with only a cryptic note left behind. The mystery of the Roanoke colony persisted to this day, inspiring multiple theories.

Archer had written ROANOKE at the top of his scratch paper and had set about testing basic keys to translating a section of the notebook. He took each apparent word in one line and divided it into its apparent "letters." A few resembled the cursive form of letters in the Latin alphabet. Others looked more like Greek or Cyrillic characters. If the whole thing was a code, the characters might correspond to characters making up English words. One common means of deciphering was noting repetitious characters and testing them against common repetitions in the English language—*ee, ll, tt,* for examples.

Two of the most common words in the English language are *and* and *the.* Archer looked for any instance of what might be a three-character word. With these two keys, it might prove possible to fill in other letters and determine other words, like solving a crossword puzzle. Archer had learned this from reading a book about the Zodiac Killer. The killer had sent coded letters to the newspaper and police, and two schoolteachers used that process to decipher one of them.

He plugged away at his key for over an hour. Nothing was clicking. None of the repetitive characters seemed to correspond to commonly repeated letters, because none of them resembled whole words in English with repetitive letters. And the few three-character words did not appear often enough or in the right places to be *and* or *the*. Most of them appeared at the end of sentences. This meant they could be other three-letter words, to be sure, but that would not help him crack the code.

It's not a code, he finally decided. All the evidence pointed the other way: it wasn't a cypher; it was another language. And while Archer was fluent in both Spanish and French, as well as passable in German, Dutch, and Portuguese, this did not resemble any language he'd ever encountered. The biggest problem, of course, was the strange characters. This language was not using the Latin alphabet, not entirely anyway. Maybe it was a linguistic hybrid of some kind, using multiple alphabets. But that's not another language. That's a code.

Unless, he thought, *it's a strange kind of dialect that combines alphabets the way some dialects combine languages.*

He looked at the word ROANOKE at the top of his musings. Certainly, it was a proper name, not a common word used for common things, but it began to grow strange in his mind. It struck his internal ear as foreign, nonsensical, like when one stares at any word too long, no matter how common, and it suddenly looks and sounds odd, even feels made up.

The word hung in his thoughts, and he tested it against other memories. And then, there it was. Another word, just as strange, just as uncommon.

Voynich.

He couldn't believe he hadn't thought of it already. There was something about the enduring mystery of the Roanoke colony that was connected to a book he'd read once about the Voynich manuscript, an old document discovered in the early 1900s that dates back to the 1400s. The unique thing about the Voynich manuscript is that it's written in an unknown language.

The pages are vellum, Archer remembered, and it was purchased from a rare-book dealer who did not recall how he came to acquire the manuscript. It's full of illustrations, too, some of which seem to correspond to known flora and fauna, but others don't seem to correspond to anything in the known world at all. Lots of people have tried to translate the manuscript. Some have deemed it an elaborate hoax. Other linguistic experts say it is too extensive and too variegated to be gibberish. It has all the markings of an actual language, albeit an otherwise undiscovered one.

Some think the Voynich manuscript was not made in this world at all, or at least not written by someone from this world.

Archer abruptly shut the green notebook. He held the cover up to his face, scanning every corner. He turned it over in front of him, examining the spine and the back. He held it perpendicular to his eyes, looking for any impressions or indentions in the surface of the cover. He inspected the inside.

There, in tiny gold letters in the bottom right corner of the inside back cover, he found this: PICKWICK.

The bookstore in town. Pickwick's Paperbacks. They had a rack of stationery, including a variety of notebooks, on a shelf near the front of the store.

So the notebooks themselves had come from right inside Echo Island itself. He fanned through the pages, letting his eyes fall across the steady stream of text inside.

These words, though. They're not from here.

It made him angry. Archer was not bothered by not knowing things, so long as they could be known. What set him off, however, was the prospect of unknowability.

She didn't seem scared at all, the girl. She stepped just inside the wall of fog and looked at Jason with peace. Like she'd been looking for him, not running from him.

Jason froze. He'd almost given up hope that they were not alone on the island, even wondered if his hope had conjured up the image of her. But here she stood, looking real enough. The first thing he noticed, in fact, was her tangibility. Wayward individual hairs departing from the combed flow of the rest, stretching out in electric defiance against the backdrop of the fog. Her dress, white as that fog but wrinkled and textured. Dimensional. The light freckles on her face and arms, the bend of her hands at the wrist against her legs. She was real. The realest thing he'd seen thus far, it seemed. At least, the most *alive*.

He said it slowly, as if speaking might spook her into disappearing again: "Hi."

She tilted her head slightly, as if it was strange to hear him speak. Or, he thought, as if she didn't understand him. But then, just as slowly and tentatively, she said, "Hi."

She is real.

The rush of all the entailments of this moment almost overwhelmed him. Jason felt his face get red. His head swam. Stars swirled in his vision. He said, "I . . ."

The girl frowned, blinked her eyes in confusion. "Are you okay?" she said.

"I . . ." Jason said. He was trying to steady himself. "I guess I don't know." He swallowed. "I think so. I just . . . I really did hope we weren't alone."

"You and the other boy?"

"Yeah," Jason said. "Boys, actually."

"I saw two of you in the store."

Jason thought for a moment. "In the grocery store? You saw Bradley and Tim, I think."

"How many of you are there?" she asked. Her eyes were blue, and at the question, a glassy shine overtook them. For the first time, she was showing something resembling fear.

"There's four of us."

She shifted her weight to the back of her heels ever so slightly.

"They scared me. I thought I was alone. When I heard their voices, I freaked out. But then I saw you later and watched you."

"You watched me?"

"Yes."

"Why didn't you say something?"

"I wasn't sure about you yet. I was scared then. But after I watched you, I realized I didn't need to be."

"Why?"

Any hint of fear was gone now. Instead she looked sympathetic, almost motherly. "Because you looked sad."

Jason was embarrassed. He certainly didn't like the idea of being spied on; he realized just how vulnerable this indeed would have made him, had she had evil intentions. And yet the fact that she was his watcher made him feel oddly cared for— not just seen but *overseen*. This, despite the fact that he had no idea at all who she was.

"How come we don't know each other?" he asked.

"I don't know," she said.

"What grade are you in?" She could not have been a year or two older or younger than he was, and while he did not know everyone at his high school, it was small enough that it was strange he'd never seen her before.

Then the alien thought occurred to him that maybe she was not from Echo Island at all, probably she wasn't even human. Given the strangeness of everything happening, why wasn't he making the obvious assumption here? This beautiful girl in the flowing white dress drifting in and out of the fog. She was a fairy of some kind, a spirit, a sprite. An angel!

"Twelfth grade," she said. "Or, I was."

"I guess you are real." He didn't mean to say it out loud.

She frowned. "What? Of course, I'm real."

"Sorry. With everything going on, I've started rethinking a lot of what I see."

"Everyone's gone," she said as if he didn't know.

"I know. Were you here?"

"Here?"

"On the island. When it happened."

"When what happened?"

"When everybody disappeared."

"Yes. I mean. Yes. But I don't know what happened."

This did not compute. How could she have been on the island and not see everything happen?

"You didn't see anything? How could you not see anything?"

"I don't know," she said. "Everything was just normal. And then it wasn't."

"Are you by yourself?"

He saw the flash of hesitation in her face. She said, "Yes."

"Are you sure?" he pressed.

"I . . ." She looked into Jason's eyes, searching for something there. His sadness she could see quite plainly, and now the intense curiosity, the eagerness for her secret. She knew he wouldn't harm her. But she wanted to make sure that she could trust him. These two things were different in her mind. "I'm alone now."

Jason could sense a world of meaning behind that statement. She had a family, just like he did. She was wrestling with their being gone, just like he was. He sensed he'd pushed too much.

He said, "We've been trying to figure it out, you know? What happened. Looking everywhere. My friend Archer—he's crazy smart. If he can't figure it out, it probably can't be figured out."

She nodded like she knew what he was talking about.

"Were you a senior last year? Or are you gonna be one this year?" he said.

"Why? Do you know everybody?"

"Kind of."

"Well, you don't know me because I didn't go to school."

"How come?"

"I . . ." She hesitated for some reason. "I was taught at home."

"Ohhh. Yeah, that's cool. But, like—I've never seen you around town."

"I was home a lot."

"Where do you live?"

"On the back end of Minuai Fields."

"I didn't know there was anything on the other side of Minuai Fields."

"Well. There is."

For some reason, she seemed embarrassed, and maybe a little irked.

Then Jason remembered there was a small mobile home park further down the road on the eastern side of the vast field. He didn't know anyone who lived there and always assumed it was an elderly community.

He wasn't sure if he should ask, but he did: "Do you want to come with me to my house? All of us are there. You know, strength in numbers and all that."

She looked across at him, the trust still uncertain. But she knew the fog could not protect either of them anyway, so she replied, "Okay."

"Um," he said. "It's back that way." He pointed over her shoulder. As if anywhere they wanted to go would require swimming across the pond behind him. "I'm Jason, by the way."

He meekly held out his hand, and after contemplating it for a second, she put her own in it, and they shook.

"I'm Beatrice," she said.

Tim was back at the Bee Market again, shopping. He wheeled a squeaking grocery cart brimming with bags of chips and boxes of cereal up and down the Bee Market aisles, wistfully eyeing each row. The comforting sights of colorful logos and perfectly photographed meals on package after package drew him steadily along. Food made him absentminded.

Tim had just reached the end of the baking goods aisle when he heard it. A clanging sound from outside. It broke his stupor, and he froze. He listened intently for a moment. There was silence, then what struck him as a scraping, like something heavy dragged across concrete.

Letting his shaky hands slip from the cart's handle, he crossed slowly to the checkout stands, stopping and wincing when his sneaker screeched on the cheap tile of the floor. He listened and could hear nothing. Bending low to avoid visibility from the windows, he made his way toward the cover of a few candy machines below the window on the far-left side of the storefront, furthest from the entrance. Carefully, he raised his head and peeked out over the red metal lids of the dispensers to spy the street outside. The fog had cleared.

The sidewalks looked empty. Tim wondered if he'd heard one of the guys, but now he was scared again and did not want to assume. He remembered the loud clang of someone in the grocery store when he and Bradley were exploring before, and he realized how stupid he'd been to go back out exploring all alone. Even Bradley out of his mind might be safer than whatever was scraping around the Echo Island sidewalks.

The thoroughfare looked as empty as it had when he came. His gaze dropping to the candy machines, he immediately became distracted contemplating the difficulty of dismantling the dispenser of the Hot Tamales. But a new sound startled him. A grunt.

He started and banged the candy machine with his knee, grimaced in pain, then froze.

There was a man on the corner of the street. A very big man. He was tall and stout with gigantic arms and huge fists clenched at his sides. A large black duffel bag sat at his feet. It was full of something.

The man was staring at the store windows, and Tim couldn't move. He couldn't tell if the man could see him peering over the candy machines, but he was afraid any movement might signal his presence. He held his pose. It was agonizing. His legs were aching, his hands shaking. His heart was racing, and he couldn't breathe.

Tim had never seen this man before. He had a thick mop of black hair and a thick, bushy beard to match. And though he was a fair distance away, his eyes looked big and black too. The man seemed to be staring right at Tim.

The moment felt interminable.

Eventually, the man glanced over his right shoulder and back up the street. Apparently satisfied that he was alone, he stooped to grab the duffel bag, which now looked very heavy, though this behemoth of a man had little trouble lifting it. He walked purposefully up the street and out of Tim's view.

The pain in his knee was especially sharp now, so Tim rocked backward to sit on his rear on the floor and stretch out his legs. But he didn't sit long. Sufficiently frightened, he carefully rose to a crouching position and hurried back to his cart. Realizing he could not be caught pushing a loaded shopping cart through the streets with that intimidating stranger lurking about, Tim stranded the cart at the head of the aisle. He receded into the rear of the store, toward the darkness of the stockrooms and kitchen. The rear exit opened into the back lot, where the loading dock was, and the woods. That way seemed much safer.

Jason did not knock at his own house. As he stepped through the door, however, Beatrice remained on the stoop, suddenly cautious about following him.

"It's okay," he said. "You'll be safe here."

She studied his face, then looked over his shoulder into the dimness of the living room behind him.

"It's okay," he repeated.

She followed, and he gently closed the door behind her.

"Do you want something to drink?" he said as they both walked to the kitchen.

There was Bradley, still at the table, his ill-gotten gains sloshed out before him.

Jason stopped cold. "What are you doing?"

"What does it look like, dum-dum? I'm—" Bradley stopped, seeing Beatrice standing slightly behind Jason. "What? Who? Oh, man." He sat up straight in his chair, feeling instantly self-conscious.

Jason said, "Dude, clean this stuff up. You can't be doing this here."

In any other circumstance, Bradley would have vehemently defended himself, but he was dumbfounded. Finally, he said to Beatrice, "Are you real?"

She softened. "Yes. I'm real."

Bradley smiled broadly, all teeth and bright eyes. "Schnikes, man, you found a girl!"

Jason said, "Yeah. We kind of found each other."

"Ohhh, man," Bradley said, now rubbing his eyes, like he couldn't believe it. "Who are you?"

"I'm Beatrice."

"Beatrice," he said. "Oh wow." He turned to Jason, "Was anybody with her?"

"No. Just her. Where are Tim and Archer?"

"Where'd you guys find each other?"

"Cutter Pond. It doesn't matter. Tim and Archer?"

Bradley chuckled to himself. "A girl, man. Holy cow."

Jason said, "Bradley!"

Bradley jumped. "Jeez. I don't know. Tim is probably stuffing his face somewhere. Archer? Who knows? Good Will Hunting on some whiteboard probably."

Jason stared at the floor, thinking. Maybe Beatrice wasn't the only other person out there. Maybe somebody else had some clue as to what happened to everybody.

Beatrice looked at the table. "Is this what you guys have been doing?"

Bradley hung his head.

"What?" Jason said. "No. This is my friend being an idiot. Where'd you even get all this?"

Before he could answer, Beatrice said, "I think we should be figuring out a way to get off the island."

Bradley perked up. "There's nothing out there. The world. Gone."

Beatrice frowned, confused.

"Yeah," Bradley continued. "I tried to paddle out there. To the mainland. Just like everything else, it just—" and he held his hands out to show the emptiness "—poof. It's not there." He laughed.

Jason said, "How much have you had?"

Bradley's head lolled back, as he looked at the ceiling in contemplation.

"What do you mean it's gone?" Beatrice asked. "The mainland's gone?"

"Well," Jason said. "We need to double-check."

Bradley straightened again. "I already checked it out, dingus. It's gone."

"That doesn't make sense," Beatrice said.

Bradley looked at Jason and gestured at Beatrice. "That's what I'm saying."

"We have to get off the island," Beatrice repeated herself.

"Yeah, maybe," said Jason. "But we need to figure out where everybody is. Or at least, what happened to everyone."

"It's an unsolved mystery," Bradley said. He was being more inappropriate than usual. "Oh, but wait." It had just occurred to him. "You were here," he said to Beatrice. "How did you not see what happened?"

"I didn't see what happened," she said. "Like I told Jason."

"You didn't see anything? How is that possible?"

"*You* didn't see anything either."

"But we weren't here," Bradley said. "We were *there*. Then we came *here*." He seemed to have confused himself. "Then, there wasn't *there* either."

Jason broke in. "We need to find Tim and Archer." Jason picked up Bradley's glass and dumped its contents in the sink. "And get rid of all this stuff."

Bradley looked incredulous. "Jason, bro, who's going to care?"

"I care. Get rid of it. At least get it out of my house. This is stupid. We aren't any closer to figuring out what's going on out there, and you're acting like nothing matters."

"Maybe it doesn't," Bradley said, but softly, like even he didn't believe it. Then he sat upright again. Something important had floated to the surface of his brain. "Oh, but wait, man. I gotta tell you something that Tim and I found. Or, didn't find, I guess."

"What are you talking about?"

"The guns are gone."

"What guns?"

"The guns, man. All the guns. Not at the liquor store. But we went to the police station. I thought, you know, it might be good to have some protection in case . . . well, I don't know, in case whatever. But there were no guns."

"The police don't just leave guns laying around the police station, you dope."

"No, man, I'm telling you. I went into the armory. There's nothing there. Not so much as a TASER. They're all gone."

Jason looked dumbly at him. He was thinking.

Bradley said, "I mean, that's weird, right?"

"It's something," Jason said.

There was a long pause. Bradley smirked with a kind of victory.

Eventually, Beatrice said, "My dad has them."

The rear door of the Bee Market was heavy and rusty, and the metallic squeal of its opening was made worse by the slowness.

Tim cautiously poked one foot out onto the concrete step. Next, he stuck his head out through the narrow gap between door and jamb. The woods were just twenty yards away. This was the same flight taken by whomever he and Bradley had frightened before. He was suddenly having second thoughts. Maybe he should hide out in the store for a while until he could be more certain that the big man had cleared the area.

But then he realized if the man was still in the area, he certainly would have heard the loud creak of the door. He was probably already heading that way, which meant Tim didn't have much time to make his escape. Every second spent with his stupid head sticking out the stupid door was another second of ground the man could gain on him.

But maybe, Tim thought. *The guy isn't an enemy at all. Maybe he can help us. He's in the same mess as we are, after all. Maybe he knows what happened.*

Or maybe he caused what happened.

The latter suddenly seemed more likely.

Tim knew he had to get back to Jason's house, find the guys, and tell them everything. If the man posed a threat, only Bradley might be big enough to match him. Tim knew for sure he couldn't defend himself alone.

He pushed the door open wider, grimacing as the creak grew louder, an ear-splitting mechanical rasp that probably meant nothing to the employees on a regular day of routine ins and outs. But to Tim, it declared, "Come and kill me."

Bolting toward the woods, he crossed the concrete and jumped up to grasp the top of the cement retaining wall between him and the trees. Tim could be strong when he wanted to be. He strained to pull himself up, using his feet against the wall to push.

Scraping his injured knee on the way up, he managed to clamber over the top and sprint into the woods. Stopping only once to catch his breath, he felt safely obscured by the brush. He panted, looking around. Finding his bearings, he realized he'd need to manage a fairly significant hike through thick brush to take the shortest route to Jason's neighborhood. The longer route would be easier, and it would avoid areas closer to the main streets and town center.

Long route it was.

Tim had taken only a few steps when he heard a loud snap behind him, a big foot on a dry stick. Whirling around, he found his face buried in the broad chest of the bearded man, who promptly picked him up and slammed him to the ground.

9

WALKING

Bradley looked at Beatrice, dumbfounded. "Your dad? Has the guns?"

"Yes."

"Like, all the guns?"

"I think so. It was one of the first things he decided to do once he realized everyone was gone."

Jason said, "Wait a minute. You said you were alone."

"I was. I mean . . . I am."

"You're not alone if your family is still around!"

Beatrice looked hurt. "He's not my family."

"He's your dad!"

"Yes."

"Wait, wait," Bradley said. "This is good. Right? He could help us."

Beatrice's hurt turned to sorrow. "No. I don't think so."

Jason touched her on the forearm, and she jerked back. "Don't touch me."

"Hold on a sec. He can't help us. And he's gathering up all the guns on the island. What exactly is he doing?" Bradley asked.

She held her arm against her stomach, holding it close with her other. "I don't know. He's not well."

"You must have some idea."

"I don't know, I told you. I think he thinks this is some kind of end-of-the-world-type thing. He's just as freaked out as you are. Only, you would not want to be around my dad when he freaks out."

Bradley shook his head. "This is some kind of nightmare."

"Where is he now?" Jason asked.

"I don't know. When he started getting strange again, I ran away. I don't want to go back home. But my guess is that if he's not out looking for supplies, he's at home."

"Minuai Fields?"

"Thereabouts," Beatrice said. "Well. Unless."

"Unless what?"

"Unless he's looking for me."

Archer had lost all sense of time. He'd stared and stared at the contents of the green notebook until his eyes hurt. All his candles had gone out, and the pale light of the lanterns wasn't helping much by this point. He needed daylight. Realizing also that he'd probably exhausted the limited resources in the historical society building, he decided to walk over to the town library.

As he walked, green notebook swinging at his side, Archer began methodically searching all the files in his mind. What had become of the Voynich manuscript? Had its cryptic text really never been solved? That's what he remembered, but it's not like he'd stayed updated on the news about it.

I really need the internet, he thought.

His head was down as he walked, deep in contemplation, hoping some hidden reservoir in his mind might give up some forgotten information. He'd been lost in his own mind before, plenty of times actually, and often came back up for air with connections even he was surprised to already know. His mother had been fond of saying that the brain is like a plastic straw, and every bit of information is like a little, hard pea stuck inside. That is, until you put a new piece of information—a new pea—into the straw. Then an old pea pops out the other side.

But Archer didn't think of his mind like that at all. If it was a straw, it was nearly infinite. Every bit of information he put in, he figured, would stay in. He could find anything he'd read, seen, heard, or experienced at any time, given enough time to search for it.

If he'd thought to look up, he'd have seen the sky was almost entirely clear now, a pale blue canvas with just three round clouds hovering above in a line like an ellipsis. Or like three white peas, perhaps.

Archer reached the library. The front door was locked. Before he looked about for something with which to break the glass, he circled the building, checking the windows and the rear exit. The library was not large; it only served a town of five thousand, after all, most of whom were not regular patrons. Archer and his mother never found the books they were most interested in there, so they were always using the interlibrary loan process. The library seemed to specialize in nature and history books, and, of course, all the most popular genre fiction that brought in most of Echo Island's thrifty readers.

The back door was locked too. But Archer discovered a low window into the basement that was unlatched. After shimmying it open, he found that he was just skinny enough to slip through.

The window was at the top of the basement ceiling, and the drop was more than he expected. He stumbled as he landed, falling over into a dusty shelf of cardboard boxes. The light streaming through the window did not provide much visibility, so with hands out in front of him, Archer felt along the passageway of shelves until he found the door to the stairwell.

The main floor of the library was easier to see, thanks to the light coming in through the front windows. Again, a short row of desktop computers mocked him. Without thinking, he stepped over to their table and shoved one of them off onto the floor.

That felt good.

He headed to where the books he read as a kid on riddles and puzzles were housed, hoping books on codes and cyphers would be there too. Scanning the shelves, though, he came up empty. The library simply wasn't large enough to include such obscure and esoteric subject matter.

What else might help? he wondered.

He surveyed all the nonfiction stacks, evaluating the subject matter by clusters, not exactly reading each spine. Nothing seemed related to the matter at hand.

Everything important these days is online, Archer fumed.

He came to the end. Six long rows of bookcases, and nothing that might help him crack the mystery text. Deflated, he sat down at the computer terminals and ruefully nudged the one he'd shoved to the floor with his foot.

He opened up the green notebook to a random page and stared again.

This has to mean something.

Outside, in the world, his friends were attempting to solve the mystery in their own ways—not thinking about the notebooks at all. Archer wondered what they were doing and if they were safe. One thing he did know: Only he was left to translate the runes. Only he had the capacity for this sacred work.

Except that he didn't.

He couldn't figure out why nothing electronic worked. He couldn't figure out where everybody went. He couldn't figure out the power station. And now he couldn't figure out the stupid notebook. He closed it.

It's not a Voynich. It's a MacGuffin.

He sighed, kicked the computer monitor on the floor. He slammed the notebook shut and threw it back over his shoulder. The pages opened as it flew, the cover, the wings of a bird descending with a flutter to the floor at the base of the fiction stacks.

He gazed out the window and finally noticed the sky was blue.

We are alone, he thought.

And then he remembered the cabin. Of course! If there were any bookcase that might help him decipher the mystery text, it would be that bookcase—the one from which he'd taken the notebook. The case was full of green notebooks. He and Jason had looked through some of them, but not all. The ones they'd inspected all contained the same indecipherable writing, but that didn't mean they all did. What if the text had been written in multiple languages? What if one of those notebooks contained a key?

He had to go back to the cabin.

But when he bent to retrieve the green notebook from the floor, the spine of a different book on the bottom shelf caught his eye.

Archer almost threw up. Coughing and sputtering, he slumped onto the floor and recoiled as if this book might jump out at him.

It couldn't be. Could it? It had to be a coincidence. How could he just happen upon this?

With a shaking hand, he pulled the book away from its snug slot among its shelfmates. He laid it in his flat palm and contemplated it, in shock.

It was a clothbound book, a brown cover with red stitching, certainly old from the looks of its design, but it did not appear to have ever been opened. And despite its color, the spine read in gold-stamped lettering: THE GREEN NOTEBOOK.

Tim had blacked out. And when he finally came to, slowly and groggily, his head was pounding. He was seeing stars, and his ears were ringing.

It was dark. For a moment, Tim thought he'd been left in the woods right where he'd been attacked, perhaps left for dead, and now night had fallen. But as he gained a bit more of his senses, he could tell he wasn't outside. The rough ground under his cheek was a scratchy carpet. There was faux wood paneling directly across from him, and as he tilted his head, he spotted the brown dust ruffle of a couch next to him.

He could not move his hands. They were tied behind him. His feet were bound too.

Now his eyes opened wide, and he craned to look every which way. He was in a narrow living space, a trailer home from the looks of the kitchen and the door, which lay about ten feet away.

He thought of yelling but decided to listen first. Was he alone? He couldn't hear anybody in the home with him.

Still, he decided not to yell. The man might be just outside.

Tim strained at his bindings. There was no slack at all. He thought maybe he could scoot himself forward, arching his back and pushing off with his bound feet against the floor. He pushed and arched, managing to scoot about six inches toward the door. His shirt caught on the floor and pulled up over his belly.

The voice came from behind him. "Where are you going, fat boy?"

Tim froze. He rolled over onto his back and looked down the length of his body. There, at his feet, sat a chair. And the large, bearded man was sitting in it.

His head was a small boulder, it seemed, and above the start of his bushy black beard sat round, fleshy cheekbones, flushed discernibly red even in the dim light of the trailer. With a fist the size of a small melon, he lifted a long gleaming knife to his jaw and gently scratched.

"I said, 'Where are you going?'"

Tim shut his eyes and began to cry.

"No, no, no. Don't do that, you big, fat baby."

Tim opened his eyes again, tears streaming down the sides of his face onto the floor.

"Don't you wet my floor, baby."

"Please, man," Tim said softly.

"Please what? Please what, now?"

"P-please. Don't."

"Don't what?" The man was smiling, a great toothy smile from behind the wiry tendrils of his unkempt beard. "Don't what?" he repeated, lowering the long blade of the knife from near his face toward Tim. "What is it you don't want me to do? I might need some ideas."

"J-just, d-don't."

Tim's hands were underneath him, tied tightly at the wrists and now pinned between his back and the floor. His shirt still bunched up near his chest, his white stomach shuddered and heaved between his gaze and the blade of the bearded man.

The man's smile disappeared. He looked angry now. "What to do?" he said.

Tim suddenly began to writhe, rolling back and forth onto his sides, kicking with his bound feet toward the man, narrowly missing the man's shins against the chair. But he had already crawled too far to make impact. He kept kicking and flopping around. Then he started yelling.

The man leapt to his feet. "No, sir!" he said, and he reached down to grab Tim by the shirt front. Yanking up, Tim's head bobbed into the air and was met by a closed fist that cracked against his skull.

Tim almost blacked out again, and as the man let go of his shirt, he fell back against the floor, his head smacking against the carpet.

He was blinking, trying to stay conscious.

"You're gonna make me do something," the man said. "Something I might not want to do. Not yet. You've got to help me, young man." He sat back down in his chair.

The knife was still in his fist, and the gleam of it caught Tim's eye. Tim was shocked he hadn't been stabbed.

"What do you want?" Tim said.

"Well, look," said the man, and he promptly slipped the knife into a sheath that hung from his belt. He clasped his hands together as if praying. "You might have noticed this place got strange. Yes?"

"I—"

"You think it's strange, right?"

"Y-yes."

"Everybody's gone. But I mean. Not everybody. I'm here. You're here. And I know there's more of you out there. So, first thing is, I want to know how many."

"How many?"

"That's what I said, son. How many?"

Tim's gut was just to tell him. *There's four of us.* Give the man all three of his friends' names, their addresses, their life histories, everything. But he knew he couldn't do that. He had to think quickly. But it was hard. His head was pounding, and he felt like he might pass out again.

"Stay with me, now," said the man. "I have ways to keep you awake, ways you won't like. How many of you are there?"

"I—I don't know," Tim said.

"How can you not know?"

"B-because. Because there's too many. I don't know everybody. How many, I mean."

The man lowered his face and glared. "There's a bunch of you?"

"Yes," said Tim. "Lots. I don't know how many."

"Guess."

Tim hesitated. "I don't know. Maybe thirty, forty."

The man looked skeptical. "No way," he said. "No way. I've already been all over this island—if that's even what it is anymore—and there's no way you got thirty or forty people stashed away somewhere."

Tim doubled down. "Well, there is. Maybe more, I don't know."

"Where at?"

"On the island."

The man stood up now in a rage. He stomped on Tim's right leg with fury.

Tim screamed.

"Shut your smart mouth and tell me the truth, son. *Where* on the island?"

"Th-the theater." He had to keep the man as far away from the Royal Garden subdivision as he could, and the theater was the only building large enough to hold as many people as he had claimed were there.

"The theater? Downtown? I looked. There's nobody."

"No, no. They were there. I went out to get food. We were scared, not sure what was happening."

"And they sent you? The big, fat baby?"

"Yes, me."

The man sat down again, shaking his head. "I guess it don't matter," he said. "Truth or not. We both know how this ends, right?"

Tim looked down the length of himself again. The man's left hand was back on the hilt of his knife.

Bradley was cleaning up the remains of his makeshift bar from the George family table.

Jason was staring at Beatrice. "Your dad is looking for you."

"I would imagine so."

"Why did you run away?"

Bradley interjected, "Man, leave her alone. People run away. Everybody's got to do what they got to do."

Jason waved his hand, as if wiping away Bradley's interruption. "Should we . . . ?" He stopped.

"Should we what?" Beatrice asked.

"Should we be afraid? Of your dad."

Beatrice said nothing.

Now even Bradley was staring at her, waiting for an answer.

Finally, she spoke. "I don't know what he'll do. He was very unnerved by everything. Started talking about the end of the world or a possible invasion. I had to get out of there. So yes. I'm afraid of him. You should be afraid of him."

Bradley sat down. He was entirely sober now. "He's got all the guns."

Beatrice said, "What do you think you could do anyway?"

"I don't know. But if he's crazy and he's armed to the teeth, it might be good to be able to protect ourselves, you know?"

Jason nodded. "He's right."

Beatrice shook her head. "No. I think we should get off the island."

"Aren't you listening?" said Bradley. "There's no place to get to."

"You don't know that!"

"Hold up," Jason said. "Let's not start that again."

Bradley looked up at him. "Man, we've got to find Tim and Archer. They're out there with this crazy guy. We have to get them back here."

"Maybe he caused this whole thing," Jason said.

Beatrice cocked her head to the side. "How would that be possible?"

"I don't know. How is any of this possible? If he's so obsessed with end-of-the-world stuff, maybe he's found some kind of device that short-circuits everything, or maybe he poisoned the water. There's got to be a reason. Somebody did this."

"My dad didn't do it."

"How do you know?"

"Because he's not smart enough, for one thing. And for another, he's just as shocked by it as you are."

"We can't just sit here," Bradley said. "We've got to find Tim and Archer."

Jason agreed. He was getting anxious now. He figured they could be in serious trouble.

"What does your dad look like?" Bradley asked Beatrice.

She looked into Bradley's eyes. Would he even stand a chance? He did look strong. But strong *enough*?

"He's big," she said. "Bigger than life. It doesn't look real, how big he is."

"Supernaturally big. Got it."

"Seriously. He's probably six-foot-six. And like, big all around too."

"Fat guy?"

"Not really. Just big."

"Roger that. Tall, big guy."

"I don't think you should be taking this lightly."

Jason said, "Bradley takes everything lightly."

"Shut it, George." Then, he looked back at Beatrice. "Very tall. Very big. That it?"

"He also has a bushy beard."

"Okay."

"And I'm telling you. He's not someone to mess around with."

"What's the name of this guy I shouldn't be messing around with?"

"Tereus."

"Tereus," Bradley said. "Never heard that one before."

Jason added, "He's got guns, Bradley."

"Right, I know," Bradley said. "We just want to find our friends. Then we can figure out what's next. But we do it together. And I want to know who I'm looking out for if I happen to run into him." He nodded a thanks at Beatrice, and then said to Jason, "You going for Archer?"

"Yeah. I'll go find him. Then we can rendezvous back here."

"Where are you going to start?" Jason said.

"Bee Market. You?"

"When Archer left, he said he was going to the power station to troubleshoot the electricity outage. That was hours ago. No electricity. My guess is he's moved on by now. And he's definitely indoors. Someplace he can find information. That really just leaves a few options: the school, the library, and the historical society."

"Or his house," Bradley added.

"He's not at his house."

"How do you know that?"

"I just do. It would remind him too much of his mom. Of the past. Of reality or whatever. Archer studies reality to avoid reality."

Bradley blinked. "That doesn't make sense."

"Well. That's Archer."

"Okay. Let's meet back here before nightfall, whether we've found them or not. Just to regroup, figure out our next step."

At the exact same time, they looked at Beatrice.

"What?" she said.

"Um," Jason said. "Do you wanna stay here? Or do you want to come with one of us?"

Bradley cleared his throat.

"I don't want to stay here by myself," she said. She looked at Jason. "I guess I'll go with you."

Jason nodded, trying to look cool.

"Whatever," Bradley said. "Don't get killed."

10

STORIES

Bradley ran in the direction of downtown, and Jason and Beatrice headed toward the coastal outskirts, where the high school was. The day had seemed interminably long by then. The sky should have already taken on the pallor of the island's dusk, but it was still blue as can be, as if the sun knew that they needed more time.

The high school was quiet and dark like every other place in town. Every door was locked. Every window looked into lifeless spaces.

"You've never been here?" Jason said to Beatrice.

"No."

"Because you were homeschooled or whatever."

"Yeah, I guess."

"Your mom taught you?"

"No."

"Your dad."

"Not really. Kinda. But not really."

"He taught you or he didn't?"

Beatrice ignored the question. "You don't think your friend is here?"

"No, I really don't. We shouldn't have come here first, now that I think of it. If Archer's doing what I think he's doing, he would not have considered the school library the best place."

"What's he doing?"

"Trying to solve the mystery. If any of us can figure out what happened, it's Archer."

Jason led her in the direction of the historical society.

The distances seemed to get shorter, the ground more easily covered. They stayed off the main roads and traipsed down alleys, through wooded areas and anywhere that might prevent exposure. Jason led the way since Beatrice was woefully and surprisingly unfamiliar with the layout of the island.

Every glance Jason stole found her returning his gaze, but while his look was curious, hers was wary. If she really had been as sheltered as she'd indicated, and if her dad really was as mean as he sounded, he couldn't begrudge her distrust. And even if neither of those circumstances had been the case, the entire scenario naturally aroused distrust on everyone's part.

But he couldn't distrust her. There was something she wasn't saying, he could tell—something mysterious about her story to be sure. But he knew she wasn't withholding out of malice.

She seemed to move effortlessly. He was in shape and yet found himself frequently out of breath. Not so Beatrice. She kept up his pace, even in her thin white flats, and she never looked like she was trying.

"Let me know if you need a rest," he said.

"I'm fine," she replied.

The statue of Virgil Grosset greeted them at the historical society building, lantern in his left hand, keys in his right, his sullen gander far over their heads, cast to worlds unknown.

The door was still unlocked.

Archer had left the lantern there, and it was still burning. At the table, Jason found *Spooky Tales of the Salty Seas* resting just under its yellow glow.

"I owned this book when I was a kid," he said.

"Was it good?"

"I don't remember."

"You don't remember if you liked it?"

"I remember I liked it. I don't remember if it was good."

Beatrice picked up the book and began to leaf through it. Jason considered each page as she turned. "I remember," he said, "there's one particular story in there I liked a lot. Something about a guy who went rowing out to sea and never came back."

"Is that spooky?"

"For kids, maybe. Or maybe it was how they told it. I don't remember all the details."

She handed him the book. "Which one is it?"

He flipped to the table of contents. Surveying the story titles, he said, "I can't tell by the names. I'm pretty sure it was in this book." He flipped through the pages himself, stopping his shuffle at random moments to see if a page jogged his memory. "Hmmm. I don't know."

"So, he just kept rowing?"

"Yeah. It doesn't sound very spooky, does it? I think there was something about his ghost coming back, maybe." Jason shut the book and handed it back to her. "It's a kid's story. It's not deep. But I liked it." He scanned the table. The only other item there was a blue pen with a NASA logo on it. "Archer was here."

"Okay, then," Beatrice said. "Where to next?"

He led her in the direction of the town library, but as they passed under the statue outside, the keys in Virgil Grosset's right hand caught Jason's eye. As they did, he noticed the power lines running overhead.

"You know, just to be sure, we should probably check the power station. That's where Archer said he was going this morning."

Soon enough, they were overlooking the rocky slope along the northern shore and the fenced-in shed and transformers of WWEC SUBSTATION 204.

At the gate, Jason called out, "Archer! Archer, are you there?"

They listened.

"Do you hear that?" he said.

"What?" she replied.

"The water. The waves on the shore."

"What about it?"

"It's the only sound left."

Beatrice was thinking. She eventually said, "I know what you mean."

"The whole island's been too quiet. You take all the people and animals away, sure, you lose noise. You take all the electronic stuff away, yeah, okay, same thing. But it's different. Other than the storm the other night, there's no birds, no wind, no nothin'."

"Quieter than quiet," she said.

"Except for the waves hitting the shore. It's like a reminder that we're still here, taking up space."

Beatrice looked herself up and down. "Yep. Still here."

Jason smiled. "You know anything about that stuff?" he said, nodding toward the transformers.

"Less than nothing."

"That makes two of us."

Jason gazed out toward the shoreline where the ocean kept coming, softly lapping at the black and gray rocks, receding in gentle streams of foam into the steadily resurgent waves. The town had officially been chartered in 1895, but those waves had been coming and going for decades, even centuries before that. The island was here long before people were. And it was still here after.

Then Jason remembered something. "There's a big cave that way," he said, pointing through a wooded rise to the west along the shore. "I haven't been down there in a long time, but my brother and the guys and I used to play around there. You ever see it?"

"No," said Beatrice. "But can we? I mean. Is it all right?"

"I think so. And maybe Archer is out there. He always liked that cave."

As they ascended the brushy knoll overlooking the northern ocean, which ran uninterrupted until the Pacific rim of Vancouver Island, he told her about the tidal pools down by the cave where he and his brother excavated crabs, starfish, and sand dollars, and the more he reminisced, the more he seemed to remember.

Beatrice was smiling at his memories. She could picture them herself.

At the top of the rise, she cleared the tree line much too swiftly for his comfort, moving too close to the edge of the cliff. He instinctively grabbed her wrist, but she shook him loose, unperturbed but, nonetheless, uninterested in his concern. "I'm fine," she said.

"Just don't stand too close to the edge. You're making me nervous."

She stood at the brim, nothing but rocky shoreline below her, looking out at the ocean. Her white dress hung limply about her frame.

The air was completely still. It made no sense.

"We can walk down this way," Jason said.

They stepped cautiously over an exposed cottonwood root since the head of the winding trail down along the face of the cliff was small, only a few square feet. This time, as Jason held out his hand to steady her, she let him. But soon, Beatrice was leading the way down, slowly and surely, balancing herself here and there by leaning against piles of rocks.

"I'm sorry about your shoes," he said.

Her white flats were muddy.

"They were already like that," she said, unbothered.

Eventually they reached the bottom. The tide was fairly high, the water gently pushing up nearly ten feet from the face of the cliff.

"It's along this way," Jason said, as he navigated over and through the tricky mounds of bowling-ball-sized rocks.

She followed until they reached the cavernous cleft in the face of the stone cliff. Storm-piled rocks had created a short barrier before the opening.

"At highest tide, I bet it fills. In a storm, you probably don't want to be in there."

Beatrice hitched her dress up slightly and lifted one slender leg over the wall of rocks, then the other. She was already walking into the gaping mouth before he himself had managed to step over.

"Your friend's not here," she called.

When he reached the top of the rock and could see in, he said, "No, I guess he's not."

"It's scary," she said, though she didn't sound scared.

"It's pretty big. I don't know how far it goes."

"All the way under the whole island, I bet."

"Maybe," he said, joining her. "We mainly played just inside here, around these little pools."

Beatrice crouched down by one of the puddles. The water was clear, and the bottom of the pool was dusted with black sand. She reached in and retrieved a polished little stone with blue and gray stripes.

"Pretty cool, huh?" Jason said.

She pondered the stone, then squeezed it in her hand. "It's real," she said. Looking all around, up and down the smooth walls to the rough ceiling above, she said, "A girl could live here."

"A girl?"

"A person, I mean."

"You'd go to bed and drown," Jason said.

"Not me," she said. "I'd float."

"Your dress would get ruined," he said.

She frowned. "That *is* something to think about."

She opened her hand to look at the stone again, and then holding it high over the tidal pond, she tilted her palm until it slid off and dropped back into the water. "But could you imagine?" she said. "You'd have the whole place to yourself, and nobody bothering you. You could make a fire. Hang some pictures on the wall. Read all you wanted without being interrupted or even worrying about anyone finding you. The world could just keep going and never know you were here."

"That sounds awful, actually."

"It sounds mysterious to me. And romantic."

"Romantic? By yourself?"

"That's not how I mean it."

He didn't know how she meant it. But he could imagine why she'd want to be alone with nobody finding her. "Are you afraid of being found? I mean, by him."

"You're bringing the world into it," she said, playfully scolding him. Then, more seriously, she replied, "But yes."

"I'm sorry."

"I don't remember a time when he wasn't like he is. Can I tell you something?"

"Yes."

"He claims my mother ran off, abandoned us. Abandoned me. But to tell you the truth, I think he did something. I honestly think he did something."

"To your mother?"

"I don't have any proof, of course. I was tiny then. I don't remember much at all. Not about her. Not about them together. But I just feel it. I think he hurt her."

"You know, you don't have to tell me all this."

"I want to. I probably need to."

Jason didn't know what to say, so he said, "I'm sorry."

"You don't have to say that," Beatrice replied. "It has nothing to do with you. And to tell you the truth, I think it's why we're here. On the island, I mean. We came, just the two of us, when I was four years old. I was born on the other side of the country. He brought me here because of what he did, I know it. But something wouldn't let him get away with it."

"What do you mean?"

"This thing, whatever is happening. It's life catching up with him. Something's catching up with him. He couldn't just start over, you know? You don't get to just run away from what you do and not have it catch up. Something is hunting him."

"Like he might be hunting us?"

"Maybe. Whatever's hunting him, whatever is the reason for all this, I have to believe is somehow . . . good."

"How can whatever or whoever did this be good?" Jason asked. "Everyone's gone. My family's gone. They might be dead."

"Maybe it was something bad. I don't know. But if it happened to interrupt my dad's desire to hide from the wrong things he's done, it has to be good. Like, as hard as he works at being so evil, there's something out there, or someone maybe, I don't know, working harder at being good. Do you believe that?"

"I don't know what you're talking about."

"That something bad could also be something good . . . or become good. I want to believe that."

"I don't know what I believe anymore," Jason said. "Everything has changed. I used to believe good wins. But that was when I thought the world ran by rules like that. Seems like the rules are out the window now."

"How should it end, then?"

"With everyone coming back. Either we figure out where they went, or they just come back. I don't know. But I wish I could go back in time and not go camping and stay here instead to see what happens. Stop it from happening. Do you think we can do that? Go back in time?"

"No."

"Why not? Seems like anything's possible right now."

"Because time travel stories never make sense. As soon as you change something in the past, the future automatically changes. Don't you see, if you go back, you might set off a chain of events that makes you not even exist."

"Like *Back to the Future*."

"Like what?"

"The movie."

Beatrice shrugged.

"I know it's old, but c'mon. It's a classic."

"I've never seen any movies. Just heard about them."

"What have you been doing all these years?"

Beatrice looked at him with immense sadness. There were things she'd seen that he hadn't, things she should never have seen.

Then she gave him the answer she could say out loud. "I've done a lot of reading."

"Time travel stories?" he joked.

"A few. Not many. My dad let me have books. I think he doesn't realize how dangerous books are. He doesn't read, which is why. But I think he also thought letting me read would keep me there, with him. But they only made me want to leave. Do you read stories like that, the ones that make you want adventure?"

"I don't read that much."

"But I bet you used to."

"Yeah, when I was younger."

"I think my favorite story is a retelling of an ancient story," Beatrice said. "It starts with a servant girl telling another servant girl a story, late at night, to pass the time and get to sleep. She tells the story of a prince who might be the son of a god, except his mother was a mortal. The other mortals are jealous of him and hate him—so much so that they begin to despise the god that he claims is his father. So they try to kill him. It goes on from there, that the god decides to kill him too—"

"His son?"

"Yeah. But he claims he won't kill him if the son can convince his fellow mortals to revere the god again. So the son goes on a series of quests—people in the old stories are always going on quests for the gods—and he has to complete a set of assignments that please his fellow mortals. And then the whole thing gets mixed up, because you can't tell if the servant girl is talking about something that truly happened or if she's making it all up. The other servant girl starts accusing her of inventing the story rather than passing it on."

"Weird," Jason said.

"You have to read it. It makes more sense. I can't retell it. It's like retelling a retelling. It loses something. But at one point, the son must go across the ocean and bring back some plant they've never seen before. And, of course, it's a magical plant that feeds and heals everybody, and they begin to like him again, which makes them like the god again."

"It sounds made up."

"It *is* made up."

"No, I mean, it sounds like you are making it up right now."

"I'm not!"

"It sounds confusing."

"It's actually very lovely."

Beatrice looked out of the cave to the ocean. She brushed strands of hair out of her face, tucking them behind her ear. "It's weird that there's waves without any wind."

Jason followed her gaze. Was the whole world really gone? There had to be something out there.

"Thank you for showing me the cave," she said.

"Of course. Around the bend up that way, there's a cool cove, as well, where we used to go paddling around. It's a pretty spot too. Archer and I went up that way to check out the view from the lighthouse."

"Should we have another look? We could see if the mainland is actually missing, like your friend Bradley claims."

"True. Then we should probably start looking for Archer again."

They climbed back up the steep trail to the top of the cliff and trekked along the elevated coastline toward the Echo Island lighthouse. The walk was long, made longer by the silence, but the day persisted, the sun apparently suspended in a Joshuaic state. When they finally reached the base of the tower, Jason's feet ached, and his side cramped.

"It's gonna be dark in there until we reach the lookout," he said. "But the staircase is pretty easy. Just hold on to the rails."

"I know how to climb stairs," she said.

"Yeah, okay." He opened the door for her and followed her into the narrow chute. They'd made one turn in the ascending spiral when the entry door shut them into the darkness. He tried to keep his distance on the climb, not wanting to bump into her, but she was moving very quickly. Jason sped up when he thought she might be too far ahead, but realized he was getting too close when he felt the brush of her dress against his knees, so he relaxed his pace.

Beatrice reached the landing at the top of the stairs, and she'd begun opening the door when he said, "Wait."

They could see each other's faces in the light through the crack. She was looking down on him on the steps beneath her.

"What's wrong?" she said.

"What if it's really not there?"

"Wouldn't you prefer to know?"

She was right. "All right," he said. "Let's see what's out there."

He squeezed in next to her on the landing, and they walked through the door together.

Jason rounded the catwalk, tracing his hand along the glass of the lantern room. He almost didn't want to open his eyes, but facing west, he did, and stared hard.

"Are you sure you can usually see it from here?" she said.

"Yes. But."

"It's not there," she said.

"It's not there."

"So, your friend isn't crazy."

"Well, Bradley *is* crazy. But he wasn't wrong about this."

He gripped the railing in his fists and squeezed.

She opened the door a little wider. "I'm tired."

"You don't look it." He was looking at her differently now.

"Okay," she said, uncomfortably.

"I'm sorry. Should I not have said that? I just meant what I said. You don't look tired."

But that's not all he meant, and she knew it.

"No, it's fine. I'm not used to talking to other people, much less having someone comment on how I look. I mean . . . hey, there's no wind up here either."

Jason paused. "You're right. There should definitely be wind this high."

"I've never been up this high."

"Oh, my bad. Are you gonna faint?"

She looked offended. "No."

Was there any figuring her out? She was as inscrutable as the island itself. None of his instincts were helping him with it, or with her.

He shifted his weight against the glass and looked back over the island. The woods stretched interminably out from their vantage point. And then again, his eye caught that thin stream of smoke rising from the northern forest.

"Should we go to the library now?" she said.

"No, there's another place Archer and I went before that he might have gone back to."

Then he told her about the cabin in the woods and the green notebooks.

"Oh, wow," she said. "That's just like in my story!"

"What are you talking about?"

"The name of the book about the servant girl who retells the ancient story. It's called *The Green Notebook*."

11

THE CABIN

Archer held the brown clothbound book in his trembling palms. He rubbed the cover. He squeezed the book, as if it might turn to smoke in his hands.

When he was sure it was real, he opened to the frontispiece, which was blank. He turned the page to find a black-and-white sketch of two girls sitting by a fire. They were in the peasant dress of antiquity, probably Greco-Roman, and they looked to be early adolescents. One girl sat on a rock by the fire, her knees hitched up to her chest, the bottom of her dress pulled taut to mid-calf. The other girl reclined on a rock opposite her, legs straight out in front of her and beside the fire, feet crossed. In her lap, she held an open book, and she gripped a quill in her right hand. There was no caption or identifying marks.

Archer turned to the title page, which consisted solely of the words *The Green Notebook* in simple block print. No author name. No publisher information. No date.

He flipped to the back cover and looked inside for the library card pocket. There was none. It was as if the book had been planted there. Just for him.

Was he going crazy?

He carried *The Green Notebook* and the green notebook from the cabin back to the table and opened the former to the first page of text, thinking, *Please be in English.*

It was. But it was not at all what he expected.

He began reading the tale of Hippodamia, who is telling a story to Ilione by their bedtime fire after a long day of slave labor. Archer was skimming quickly, trying to get the gist. Hippodamia's tale was about a demigod named Meleager. His mother was a slave, and his father was rumored to be a god. Apparently, Meleager was quite proud of this rumor, and he boasted of it constantly, to the point of turning even his friends into enemies.

On and on he read, but Archer felt like he was missing something. The book wasn't telling him anything he wanted to know.

He stopped a few pages in, and he opened up the green notebook, once again staring at its cryptic text. Was this the same book in a different language?

Perhaps the notebooks held a translation of the book. Maybe the author was experimenting in code. Or maybe the book was an English translation of what had originally been handwritten in the notebooks.

Archer thought back to that bookcase in the cabin. There were way too many notebooks to translate to this relatively short tome on the table in front of him.

Or maybe it was just a coincidence. The odds of the green notebook landing next to a book called *The Green Notebook* had to be astronomical. And yet it had happened. Just like the disappearance of the whole town and the complete shutdown of anything electronic; it had happened.

This means something, he thought. But he had the overwhelming feeling that the strangeness was outrunning him. The deeper he went, the more disorienting it became. He had never experienced this before. The mystery was getting bigger, not smaller.

He read a few more pages. Meleager was about to be burned in a fire by a town mob, when an unseen hand swooped down and saved him. It was his father, the unnamed. He told Meleager that he had not enjoyed the town's devotion and offerings since having his good name soiled by the scandalous rumor mill turning on and on about gods consorting with mortal women. He claimed he was going to kill Meleager himself, but he decided he wouldn't, so long as Meleager could turn the hearts of the citizens back to him.

Every ten pages or so, the story would pause as the scene returned to the teller, Hippodamia, and to the hearer, Ilione. Hippodamia would ask Ilione if she was understanding the story, if she was liking it, or if she wanted Hippodamia to stop. "No, no," Ilione kept saying. "I want to hear more." Hippodamia then resumed, plunging the narrative back into the hero's tale.

Archer flipped through the rest of the pages. This pattern repeated throughout the book, punctuating the heroic exploits of Meleager at land and sea to reclaim the goodwill of his countrymen and the cosmic pardon from his father. The story didn't interest him much, and the conceit of the girl telling it seemed strained. And none of it seemed to explain anything about what was going on with him and his friends on Echo Island.

In any event, Archer's problem was that he could not test this text against the mystery text of the handwritten notebook. He'd pulled the notebook he'd been studying at random off the shelf.

If he had the first notebook or even the last, he could compare it to the opening and closing of the story. If the notebooks were indeed translations or even proto-versions of the story, he might be able to identify that in the comparative paragraph lengths or sentence word counts. Of course, no translation is word-to-word in its correlation, but it was better than nothing.

Archer knew what he had to do: get back to the cabin and the rest of the notebooks.

Surprised by the enduring daylight, he plodded north to the coastal cliffs, cutting across streets, parking lots, and yards. The journey seemed to take no time at all. When he reached the edge of the forest, he could barely remember passing landmarks he had most assuredly passed.

Deeper and deeper Archer pressed into the wooded expanse, wading through brush and traversing fallen trees and risen roots.

He'd no sooner stepped his long legs over a mud puddle when he thought he heard a footfall behind him. He froze. Listened. Nothing stirred, not even leaves in the breeze.

Satisfied he'd only imagined the steps, Archer took his own step forward when suddenly that low, moaning roar came through the trees. It was the same sound he'd heard in the same woods when he'd come before with Jason. It sounded like it had come from the oceanside, from outside the woods, in fact. What was it? A bear? Something larger?

He didn't stop to find out but kept walking until he came once again upon the stone cabin. Like *The Green Notebook*, it didn't seem to belong, not where he found it nor on the island at all.

The chimney was still issuing smoke, a thicker plume now than before. Somebody was there. Or had been.

Archer knocked twice. Then three times, louder. Satisfied that once again no one was home, he opened the door a crack and peered in. Seeing nothing, he opened it all the way and stepped inside.

The space looked as he and Jason had left it. The furnishings had not moved an inch.

There was no open work on the desk, and the butts in the ashtray did not warm his hovering hand.

Embers still glowed in the fireplace, however, which meant that whoever lived here was still on the island, still feeding the fire from time to time. The idea that the fire had been smoldering since the disappearance was ludicrous. It was his first definitive discovery in the pursuit of the mystery. They weren't, in fact, alone.

And that is when he heard footsteps on the narrow porch outside, and the door, which he'd left cracked, creak softly behind him. He turned in fright.

"I thought you'd be here."

It was Jason. And a girl.

"What?" Archer said, dumbfounded. "Who?" He gestured at her.

Jason stepped into the dim light. He gave Archer an enthusiastic hug, though Archer's arms hung limply at his side.

"I'm glad you're okay, man," Jason said. "This is Beatrice. She lives on the island. We sort of found each other."

Archer craned his neck to the ceiling, as if his confusion might be vanquished from on high. Finally, he looked at Beatrice again. "Do you live *here*?"

"No."

"What happened to everyone?" he asked.

"She doesn't know," Jason said. "She's as clueless as we are. Did you find anything?"

There was a deep well of sadness behind Archer's eyes. "I—I don't know. I really don't know. I thought I did. I tried and tried to decipher one of the green notebooks, and then I found another book literally called *The Green Notebook.* I don't know if it has anything to do with anything, or if I'm just going crazy."

"I know that story," Beatrice said. "It's my favorite."

"Yeah?" Archer said. "Well, it's driving me insane. I came back here to look into more of the notebooks. Maybe there's something here, but I'm beginning to think whatever is happening is beyond figuring out."

Jason took two steps forward. "Don't say that, man. We've got to figure out something."

Beatrice said, "We need to figure out how to get off the island."

"You haven't told her?" Archer said. "Our idiot friend says there's nothing out there anymore."

Jason looked at Beatrice knowingly, then said, "Archer, it's true. We went up to the lighthouse and looked out. The mainland's gone."

"It can't be."

"But it is."

"There's no logical explanation," Archer said. "What if this isn't even what we think it is? What if we're not even on Echo Island?"

"Where else would we be?"

"I don't know!"

Beatrice jumped.

"Sorry. I mean," he said gently, "I don't know. But there are some theoretical physicists who suggest the whole world we live in might be a simulation."

"What does that mean?"

"It means that it's possible that everything we experience as life is really just a supremely advanced computer simulation orchestrated by some exterior force."

"What kind of force?" Beatrice asked.

"I don't know," said Archer. "Extraterrestrials or something. It doesn't matter. But what if this is all a weird Matrix-type thing? Or a dream even?"

Beatrice said, "What's the Matrix?"

Archer stared at her pitifully.

"It doesn't feel like a dream or a simulation," Jason said. "It feels real."

All three of them jumped when a deep voice from the doorway said, "Because it is real."

Bradley rounded the corner near the Bee Market and stopped to catch his breath. If Tim were still wandering, he'd probably be in there, but Bradley opened the door cautiously, not remembering if there was a bell above the door.

There wasn't. The grocery store was dark. Bradley listened intently for any sound. If Tim were in there, he might be transfixed in the cereal aisle. Tim had always had a thing for colorful food packaging.

Bradley crept lightly around the aisles, looking around the endcap displays carefully and down each row. No sign of Tim.

Bradley inhaled deeply and exhaled slowly. He'd already decided his next plan of action: cross Minuai Fields where Beatrice said she lived with her dad.

He walked through the woods around the circumference of the open field. If Tereus was as dangerous as Beatrice had said, and if he was armed to the teeth, approaching in the wide open was probably not a great idea.

On the northwest corner of the fields, at the tree line, which was nearest the coast, Bradley began walking east along a ridge. The soft roar of the waves below was more pronounced, given the lack of wind. And when he had crossed the entire expanse of the northern edge of the field, he could see down an embankment. In the midst of an acre of level and grassy ground stood a mobile home. He wondered why he'd never noticed it before.

He hunched over and crept along a low border of brush that ran around the back side of the trailer. He figured knocking on the front door was probably not a good idea.

I can be smart, Bradley thought to himself.

When he was at the midway point of the rear of the home, he crouched backward into the brush and watched. There were two windows on the rear of the building, but both sets of blinds were closed. He couldn't hear any noise, but he was still quite a ways across the yard.

Bradley knew he had to get closer. So he got down on his hands and knees and started crawling.

I am not smart, he thought to himself.

He reached the base of the trailer, which was elevated on blocks, the gap below covered with a wide strip of white lattice along the bottom. He rose to his feet but bent at the waist to keep his head below the level of the windows.

He put his ear against the vinyl siding, but still he heard nothing.

It took him a few minutes to work up the courage, but eventually Bradly lifted his head to window level. The sill was barely at the height of his eye, but he could see from the corner through the slightest crack in the blinds.

He stopped cold.

There was a figure sitting on what looked to be a couch, facing the window.

The person just sat there. Maybe he couldn't see him. But Bradley was afraid to move.

He strained his eyes, trying to make out any features, but the interior was too dark. The shadow and he were in a staring contest. Who would break first?

The shadow did. A slight tilting of the head sideways. Bradley jumped back away from the window but bumped his head against the side of the house. He froze, listening for the rush of footsteps on the trailer floor.

Instead, what he heard was a mournful moan from inside the trailer, a guttural warble he'd recognize anywhere. It was Tim.

Suddenly he had to be inside the trailer. But the front door was the only way in.

Bradley quickly scanned through the crack in the blinds again. He couldn't see anyone else in the room, though it was dark, and his perspective was too narrow to be sure. He could see Tim's silhouette leaning now.

"All right," Bradley whispered to himself. "Okay." And then he brazenly walked around to the front of the trailer and turned the flimsy knob on the thin door. He opened it slowly, halfway expecting to be riddled with gunfire.

When nothing happened, he entered the trailer. The light coming in through the door gave him a clear view of the long layout, and of Tim tied at the feet, hands behind him, sitting on the couch. His face was bruised and bloody, and there was duct tape wrapped around his head and covering his mouth.

Bradley rushed over to him. "Oh man," he said. "What happened to you?"

Tim jumped, eyes wide. He had expected Tereus.

Seeing Bradley on his knees feverishly untying the binding around his ankles, he began to cry.

It took a fair bit of untangling, but soon Tim's feet were free. Bradley then went straight to the duct tape and pulled it down below his friend's mouth. It ripped as the adhesive tore his skin.

"What happened?" Bradley repeated.

Tim gasped for air. "Huge guy," he sputtered.

"We need to get you out of here."

"He's going to kill us all."

Bradley pushed Tim over to the side, trying to get at the binding on his wrists.

"Can you walk?" he said.

"I don't know," Tim replied.

"Can you run?"

"I don't know."

"Well, you're going to have to."

Bradley heaved one of Tim's arms over his neck and hoisted him up off the couch. He practically dragged him to the front door, and as they reached the tiny wooden landing of the few steps down to the yard, he stopped abruptly. The biggest man he'd ever seen was sauntering down the embankment from Minuai Fields. The man had seen them too and froze.

"Here we go," Bradley said.

The sight seemed to catch Tereus off guard. He puzzled for a second, unsure what he was looking at. It was enough time for Bradley to get down the steps, Tim practically hanging onto him, and start for the side of the trailer. He had to get the trailer between them and Tereus because the man had a rifle slung over his shoulder and was now bringing it up to ready.

They had just reached the corner when the report exploded in the air. A bullet struck the side of the trailer by Bradley's neck with a hollow thud. He found strength he didn't know he had, and the gunshot seemed to inspire Tim to find more as well. They scrambled around the side of the house.

They could tell by the heavy footsteps that Tereus was running after them now.

Jason, Beatrice, and Archer whirled around. There, in the doorway to the cabin, stood a man none of them had ever seen before, yet who carried with him an air of familiarity. He was neither tall nor short, but jovially plump, especially in his reddish face, bald with a thatch of black hair around the back of his head, wearing flannel-cloth pants and a tweed coat over an off-white, button-up shirt.

"Is that—?" Jason began.

Beatrice read his mind. "No." It was not her father.

As if reading all of their minds, the man said, "You can call me Jack." He spoke with an English accent, but more striking still was the pleasant deepness of his voice.

"Who are you?" Archer asked.

"Why, I've just told you," said Jack. "And what a thing to ask after you all barged into my home."

"This is your cabin?" Jason said.

"For the moment, yes." He closed the door behind him, and for the first time they each noticed he was carrying a black walking stick with a silver knob on the end, which he gently laid against the wall by the doorframe.

Jack began to take off his coat. "Still. I was expecting you," he said.

"You were expecting *us*?" said Jason.

"Certainly. You weren't expecting me?"

"How do you mean?"

"You come into a man's home, rifle through his things, and mull around without expecting he'll come home?"

"We thought everyone was gone."

"Most everyone," said Jack. "But you're here. And so am I."

"Do you know what happened?" Archer said.

Jack looked at the boy, considering all angles and points of his face. They couldn't have been more different. "What have you got there in your hand?"

Archer was clutching the green notebook he'd earlier taken from the shelf and the copy of *The Green Notebook* he'd taken from the library.

"What did they tell you?" Jack asked.

"Nothing," Archer said. "I don't know. I don't understand them."

Jack looked at the boy with undeniable sympathy. "I suppose it isn't time." He crossed to the desk and, pulling away the chair, sat down and began to unlace his shoes.

"Have you always lived here?" Jason said. "I've never seen you before."

"I've never seen you before either." He pronounced *either* with a long *i*, like eye-ther. "Have you always lived here?"

"Yes."

"Well, I'll admit I have not. In a manner of speaking, I am just passing through. But then, in a manner of speaking, so are you."

"Look," Archer said. "Who are you? What are you doing here?"

"In the woods, do you mean? In this cabin? I'm a writer. It's a lovely place to write, don't you think? It's quiet. Rather secluded. When I'm very still, I can hear the ocean. And when I'm restless, the walks are splendid."

"What do you write?" said Beatrice.

"Oh dear, all kinds of things. Poetry, philosophy, stories. I have written in as many categories as you might name."

"Stories?" Beatrice asked.

"Yes, stories. They *are* my favorite."

She smiled.

Archer stepped up to the bookcase with the array of green notebooks. "Did you write these?"

Jack reached out for the notebook in Archer's hand, which the boy slowly gave to him. Jack leaned over to the case, inspecting it for the proper gap and, finding it, slipped the missing piece back into its slot on the shelf. Sitting back, he pondered the rows of notebooks for a moment, and finally said, "Yes. I wrote them. You could put it that way. Though I am more like a secretary for their contents."

"What does that mean?"

"It means, my dear boy, that the writing is mine, but the telling isn't."

"What kind of language is it?"

"The kind that takes some time to understand." Jack smiled. "Now," he said, clapping his hands together, "why don't you each have a seat? There are things we must talk about."

"I'm not sitting down until you tell us what's going on," Archer said.

"I cannot tell you straightaway," Jack said. "But you will know."

Jason sat down on the stone hearth and brushed off a spot for Beatrice. Straightening her dress beneath her legs, she sat beside him. Archer remained standing.

"These notebooks. They mean something, don't they? I mean, they're not just gibberish."

"Certainly not," Jack said. "I have never in my life committed any length of time to gibberish."

"So, what does it mean?"

"I'm afraid, as I said, that I can't tell you. I have not been sent to tell you everything. At least, not in the beginning. I'm here to be your guide, to help you understand."

"Sent?" Jason said. "Sent by who?"

"By *whom*," Jack said. "And we shall get to that page soon enough."

"The whole world's gone crazy," Archer said. "This is unreal."

"You keep saying that," Jack said. "Or thinking it. As if you have any conception of what is more or less real in the first place. You imagine your world before things became inexplicable was more real and this world less so. But what if, in fact, it's the other way around?"

"Is that a riddle?" Beatrice said, delighted at the prospect.

"My dear, to some it has been given to know the secrets, but to others it has not been given."

Archer was not listening. Absentmindedly thumping *The Green Notebook* against his leg, he could not take his eyes off the bookcase.

"I want to see," Beatrice said. "What do I do?"

"You must think hard on that great divide between what you sensed was real and what you think is not. Where was the line drawn? One moment you lived as you did, and now you live as you are. What happened?"

"That's what we're asking you," Jason said. "We don't know."

"What's the last thing you know?"

"The whole island had more people! Cars worked. Clocks worked. Everything worked! There was a whole country there, and now it's gone."

Jack looked at Beatrice. "You aren't so sure, are you?"

"I don't know what you mean."

"You aren't so sure that *that* wasn't the dream."

Jason said, "I had a family. *Have* a family. And they're gone. Where did they go?"

Archer finally interjected. "Enough with the riddles, grandpa. Tell us what happened."

"You're a hard one, aren't you?" Jack said. "I've already told you I can't just give you the answers. Not straightaway. Not yet."

"Can't? Or won't?"

"Properly speaking, both."

"So you don't want to give us the answers? You don't want to help us?"

"I'm not able to want to. But even if I was able to *want* to, I still could not."

"I just didn't think this could get any weirder," Archer said, exasperated.

"Let's try it this way," said Jack. "You tell *me* what happened."

"But we don't know," Beatrice said. "That's just the thing. That's why we're asking you."

"No, no. I mean, just before all of this. What happened? What is your last memory of life as you knew it?"

The room grew quiet. Beatrice stared at the wood floor. Finally, she spoke, "I remember. I remember that my father was angry. I mean, he's always angry. But he was especially angry. I remember him tearing about the house. He broke a glass in the sink. Just smashed it away right there into the sink. Bits of glass everywhere. He was shouting and . . ."

"Yes?" said Jack.

Jason looked at Beatrice's face. A teardrop was swelling in the corner of her eye.

Meekly, she whispered, "I think I told him I was going to go away. I couldn't live there any longer. I had done all I could to love him into something different. I wanted to. But I could see it wasn't going to work. Or, you know, if it was going to happen, it wouldn't be because of me. I think that's right. I think I said I wanted to leave."

"That's the last thing you remember?" Jason asked.

"He did . . ." She hesitated. "He did something awful."

THE CABIN

Jack pulled a folded handkerchief from his pocket and handed it to her. Beatrice was practically curled up onto herself, her head nearly in her lap. She dabbed at her eyes behind the waterfall of hair that now obscured her face. Almost inaudibly she simply said, "He hurt me."

She rose slowly then and gave Jason a mournful look before crossing the room and exiting the door.

"Should we go after her?" Jason asked.

"No," said Jack. "She is composing herself. Give her a moment. But what of you lads? What do you remember?"

Jason looked at Archer, who was again staring at the bookcase.

"I don't know," Jason said. "We were camping. On the mainland. It was the last day. We were just heading back home. That was it."

"We crashed," Archer said, still not averting his gaze from the notebooks.

Jason looked at Jack. "That's right. I almost forgot. We got in a crash. In Bradley's jeep."

He replayed everything in his head. The deer running out. The jeep careening over. Hanging upside down. The phones not working.

Before he said another word, Beatrice returned. Her eyes were still damp, but she was no longer crying. Jason continued. "After the crash, we started walking back."

"The ambulance," Archer said.

"Oh, right," said Jason. "The ambulance blew right by us."

"Just like . . ."

"Yeah. Just like we weren't even there."

Archer and Jason looked at each other. Their faces said, *No. That can't be it.*

161

The boys looked at Jack. The man was grinning, coaxing them on from the desk chair with his relaxed demeanor.

It couldn't be that.

"It can't be," Archer said out loud.

Even the stupid ferryman, thought Jason. *He was wearing a Styx shirt. It couldn't be more obvious.*

The boys turned the corner of the trailer. Tereus was running down the yard after them. They had only seconds to make a move.

Bradley knew they couldn't clear the ground between the trailer and the woods before their pursuer would catch sight of them. He'd shoot them both in the back before they could even reach the tree line.

Pure instinct was kicking in. If Bradley was exceptional at anything, it was fighting.

Looking down, he saw the white lattice at the bottom of the trailer. Without thinking, he reached down, grabbed hold of it, and pulled. A section gave way. *I may not be that smart, but I am strong,* he thought. He shoved Tim down. "Crawl," he ordered.

Tim did not think to object. He wondered if he'd get caught under the trailer and be a sitting duck, but he promptly obeyed. His body felt numb from his captor's abuse, but he wriggled quickly under the trailer. He kept crawling on his belly and forearms, toward the front of the house, farthest away from where Tereus was about to end up.

Bradley had two choices now. Make a break for the far end of the trailer and try to outflank the man, using the building as cover, or stay put. He decided to stay put, crouching down by the corner of the trailer, hoping his pursuer would come recklessly close to the side of it.

He did. Assuming the boys were making a break for the woods, Tereus darted along the side of the trailer at full speed. Right when he heard the closest footfall and the huffing of the man's breath, Bradley launched himself, thick shoulder first, up and out into the man's rib cage as he passed. Football seemed like a distant memory now, but it felt good to hit a man again.

There was a gentle crack in Tereus's ribs and a loud *whomp* as he careened sideways and hit the ground.

He did not stay down long. No sooner had Tereus skidded to a stop in the grass than he was already clambering back up.

Bradley ran around to the front of the trailer. He remembered the guns.

He raced to the porch and through the door, shutting it behind him. To his surprise, Tim was inside.

"What on earth, man? I told you to go under!"

"I did. But I came back inside."

"No duh. What are you doing?"

Tim was holding a kerosene lantern he'd found under the trailer in one hand and a lighter he'd grabbed off the kitchen counter in another. "I'm gonna burn the place down."

"Not with us inside it, Biggie Smalls."

Tim cocked his head.

"Did you see any guns?" Bradley said.

"I don't know," Tim said. "Maybe in there?" He was pointing to a door at the end of the living room.

The sound of footsteps quickly ascended the porch.

Bradley made a break for the bedroom. Tim ducked down behind the small counter that separated the open kitchen from the living room.

Tereus kicked the door open just as Bradley darted inside the bedroom. If the man hadn't heard the bedroom door just as it shut, he might have turned to his right and easily discovered Tim slumped behind the kitchen counter armed only with a lamp.

Tereus lumbered toward the bedroom, rifle ready. But he stopped at the door.

Bradley was on pure adrenaline now. He didn't even stop to marvel at the fact that he'd just jumped into the most stocked armory he'd seen in his life. The floor, the bed, the dresser— every space was covered in firearms of every kind. He didn't hesitate but grabbed the first thing he saw, a pistol.

Bradley pressed his back against the wall just to the right inside the door.

They listened to the sound of each other's heavy breathing on either side of the wall.

"Listen, kid," Tereus finally said. "Come out and show me your hands. I'll let you and your friend go."

Bradley said nothing.

"You don't want the alternative; I promise you that. You don't want to know what I will do if you don't come out."

Bradley's hand was sweating on the gun handle. He wondered if it was even loaded.

"All right," Tereus said. "Have it your way."

He stepped back and with an easy kick, popped the door open.

Bradley instantly turned with the gun and pulled the trigger. Click, click, click. It wasn't loaded.

Tereus burst through the door, rifle barrel first. Bradley quickly ducked under it and, springing himself forward, knocked the man onto his heels and against the fallen door. As he stumbled back, Bradley angled through the bedroom door and made a break for the front door again, yelling as he went, "Tim, if you can hear me, run!"

A shot rang out as he burst through the door to the outside, chips of siding spraying against his face. He leapt from the steps and tore off for the woods.

Another shot rang out, and a bullet whizzed by his head as he sprinted.

But then, he heard something else. An abrupt yelp. Something. Against all instincts, he stopped and whirled around.

Far away on the small porch landing to the trailer home, something was happening. It took him a second to register what he was seeing.

Tim.

He was still in the trailer.

And there was a blaze of fire emanating from the doorway. The door was somehow on fire. But not just the door. The man. He had turned toward the opening, and his entire back was ablaze. He was screaming and walking back into the house.

No, no, no. Bradley started running again, this time toward the house. *Tim, what did you do?*

He'd almost reached the wooden steps up to the door when the door, windows, and siding burst open with an enormous rush of hot air licked by flames. Bradley was blown back onto the ground.

The fire was rapidly catching, the flames rushing all along the structure, when out from the blazing doorway staggered a blackened figure.

"Tim," Bradley said.

But by the sheer size, Bradley could tell it wasn't Tim.

Jason felt sick to his stomach. His head was dizzy. He reached over beside him on the hearth and placed a shaky hand on Beatrice's arm.

Archer sighed loudly. "This is impossible."

Beatrice said to him, "Just think about it."

"That's all I've been doing!"

Jason looked up at his friend. Softly, he said, "Archer, just calm down."

"If you guys want to believe this craziness, I can't stop you. But there are theories, and there are facts. There are things we can see and hear and touch and taste. There is, you know, *reality*. And I don't know what's happening, but this guy's taking you on a trip away from reality. It's not possible."

"Archer," Beatrice said, "stop."

"No. *You* stop, strange girl who showed up like this strange guy to make everything confusing."

Beatrice shrank back, hurt.

Archer cried out, "Too many variables!" before he began grabbing notebooks off the shelf. He removed the first three and tucked them under his arm, keeping a wary eye on Jack, who remained seated at the desk, watching him, apparently unbothered.

Then Archer bolted for the door.

Jason called after him. But his friend was gone.

"Some things are meant to be calculated," Jack said. "Mystery isn't among them."

"Are you just going to let him take those?" Jason said.

"He has already taken one notebook from the shelf before. Once he'd done that, it was inevitable he'd want more. In any event, I cannot stop him."

"Is it true?" said Beatrice.

"What, dear?"

"Are we actually . . ."

"Yes?"

"Are we dead?"

"Oh," Jack said, "it's not as simple as all that."

12
REVELATIONS

The day had felt interminably long, but night fell suddenly. The moon was like an ivory comma over quiet woods and empty streets, as if the whole island had more to say.

Archer did not seem to notice. He rushed back to the library, three green notebooks clutched to his chest. He was not afraid of any threat still looming on the island. He was not concerned about the whereabouts of Bradley and Tim. He had barely thought of his mother. He only wanted to know what the notebooks said.

Now, while the truth seemed to be slipping from his grasp, he had to redouble his mental efforts in possessing it. This man Jack was a discombobulating presence. His theory didn't fit with anything Archer knew about the known world. Already, Archer knew he was having to account for more and more strangeness in his figuring—making the likelihood of a logical explanation for everything more and more *un*likely—but the sudden appearance of a riddle-telling Englishman in a mysterious cabin in the woods was a bridge too far. The oddities were accumulating too quickly.

He returned to the table in the library, lit a lamp, and cracked open the very first notebook from the bookcase, straining over the strange text. Next to it, he opened *The Green Notebook*, comparing the first sentence of each. In terms of word count—if the arrangement of symbols in the green notebook were words at all—the sentences did not even come close to matching. The first sentence of the novel was exactly eleven words long:

Two servant girls by firelight each night told each other stories.

The opening sentence of the green notebook appeared to constitute the length of a short paragraph.

Archer scanned each word, each line, skimming every sentence as naturally as possible, not stopping on each word or thinking too much about how the symbols might translate to the English alphabet. He kept this up for three or four pages when something remarkable began to happen. It was as if the words were shifting before his very eyes. The effect was similar to those optical illusion paintings that, on the surface, simply look like a chaotic swirl of color—that is, until the looker both focuses *and* relaxes. Then in that strange, undefined, visual sweet spot—the presence beneath or beyond the chaos—some definable object is revealed.

The text was transforming before his eyes, becoming intelligible.

He could read it.

She said, "What did you mean it's not as simple as all that? Are we dead?"

"In a manner of speaking, yes. The four boys died in that car accident."

"No," Jason said.

"And you—" Jack said, still looking from his seat at Beatrice.

"I think I know now," Beatrice said. "My father . . . killed me."

Jason stood up from the fireplace. "What? No. None of this can be true."

"It is, young man," Jack reiterated. "But your deaths are only one part of the story. There are more important things for you to understand."

Jason erupted. "What on earth are you talking about? You've just told us we're all dead—that Beatrice has been murdered even—and we've been floating around on this island like ghosts? Is that right? It's not that everybody else is gone. We are! We're the ones who are gone. And what does that make this place? Hell? What?"

"It is not hell."

"Well, it's not heaven either, is it?"

"No, it most certainly isn't heaven."

"Help us, man! Tell us what's going on. If this isn't heaven or hell—and it sure isn't Echo Island—where are we?"

"But it *is* Echo Island. That is, Echo Island as it was meant to be. When you crossed over the river Styx, in a sense, the island did as well. And it is just as real as you are. In a way, it is *more* real than it was before, just as you are."

"How can we be more real? Aren't we ghosts?"

"Do you feel like a ghost?"

"Well. No, not exactly."

"You aren't a ghost."

Beatrice was watching the entire exchange from her seated position at the hearth, looking plaintively up at them as they spoke. She was about to speak when they heard a loud banging on the door.

"Archer?" Jason called out.

"No!" the voice replied, and the door opened. It was Bradley. He was covered in sweat and dirt and was clearly out of breath.

"And next, I caught a glimpse of powerful Heracles," Jack said.

Jason met him halfway across the floor. "What happened?"

"Tim," Bradley sputtered. "Tim's . . ."

Beatrice finally rose. "Oh no."

"He's dead. The man in the house. There was a fire. And Tim's gone."

Jason grabbed him by the shoulders, "Bradley, what happened?"

"It was awful, man."

Jason saw fear in Bradley's eyes. It was not a common sight.

"He tried to kill me."

"Tim?"

"No, no. The guy. Her. Her dad."

Jack calmly said, "Tereus."

"Yeah," Bradley said. And then it struck him that there was a bald man he'd never seen before sitting coolly beside him. "Who are you?" Then to his friends, "Who is this?"

"You can call me Jack."

Bradley shook his head as if he could reset the whole timeline, jostle everything out of his brain.

Jason recaptured his gaze. "Bradley, what happened to Tim?"

"That guy, Tereus, he had Tim tied up in his house. I managed to get Tim out, but Tereus just started shooting. And Tim, Tim didn't make it." Then, he said angrily, "That idiot. I told him to crawl under and run away. And he never listens. I have to do everything for him!"

Beatrice spoke up again. "Did my father . . ."

Bradley stopped. He looked at her, anger gone and fear returning. "Yeah. I don't know. I was outside. I thought Tim was already in the woods maybe. I don't know—it happened so quickly. And when I turned around, the whole thing was on fire. And your dad, he came walking out of there." He swallowed. "Like a demon or something."

He was breathing slower now and wiped his hand across his wet brow.

"I just started running," he said. "Trying to get away. Ran into the woods. I didn't know if he was following or not. But I just kept running. And somehow, I ran into this place."

"Somehow," Jack said.

Jason grabbed hold of Bradley's arm. "Tim?" he said.

Bradley looked him in the eyes. Jason had never seen him sad, not since they were little kids. "Yeah," Bradley said. One small tear dropped from his eye.

Jason swallowed, lowering his head toward the ground.

"I am sorry," Jack interjected.

Bradley wiped his cheek. He looked over at the man, stared at him for several seconds, and then said, "Who are you again?"

Jason replied for him, wiping a tear from his own face. "This is Jack. He says he's our guide."

"Our guide to what?"

"That's what I'm beginning to wonder," Jason said. "Guide to what? Because you just said we're all dead, and our friend Tim just died. How do dead people die?"

"All in good time," Jack said.

"Wait," said Bradley. "We're *dead*?"

"Yes," Jack said, "but as I said to your friends, this is not the most important thing to know."

"It seems pretty dang important." Bradley stared at the floor. "Man. This actually makes sense. The jeep, right? When we crashed."

"Yeah," Jason said.

"Good grief, it makes sense. That's why everyone's gone. We thought everybody disappeared, but really it was us."

The room fell silent.

"But wait, if we're dead," said Bradley, "then where are we?"

Jack replied, "I was just getting to that when you arrived. That you have died is what has happened. But that is simply the premise for where you find yourself at the moment. It is not *the story*."

Bradley looked at him. "Is this how you always talk?"

"There's only so much I can say," said Jack. "Whenever possible, it is better to show than to tell."

"But at least tell us if we're in purgatory," Beatrice said.

"No," said Jack. "Purgatory, properly speaking, does not exist."

"But you said it's not heaven or hell either. *Is* there a heaven and a hell?" Jason asked.

"Most certainly."

"Then where are we?" all three of them asked.

Jack sighed. He looked up to the ceiling for a moment, as if receiving a word. Then he looked at each one in turn—Bradley first, then Beatrice, and finally Jason. Uncrossing his leg, he folded his hands in his lap and said, "You are in a construct. You might say, a *supposal*."

"What does that mean?'

"It means, my dear, that you are in someone else's imagination."

Archer was afraid to stop, afraid that if he did, the words would go away. He could read them. And what he read was startling, striking him to the heart. He couldn't believe his eyes, but he dared not blink.

He could read the words in the notebook plain as day. He read:

Like clockwork, like the tipping of that scale, the island slowly rose from the sea, taking its jagged shape of rocky beach and angular forest. Eventually, the beach ran as far east and west as he could see, and the ferry's bumpered hull gently rubbed against the concrete dock. The ferryman descended the cabin without a word, locked the vessel to the broad boat ramp, and lowered the gate, which usually withstood the passage of cars, but that morning only upheld the unloading of the foursome.

It was a description of the route between the mainland and Echo Island. But it seemed even more specific than that. It seemed *personal*. Yes, it was *their* route.

Archer kept reading, undeterred by the shock that slowly overtook him as he quickly discovered the notebooks were chronicling everything that they'd been doing from the end of their camping trip forward. All of them were in there—Jason, Bradley, Tim, himself.

He flipped forward several pages and read:

"Power goes out all the time."

"Yeah, okay," Bradley mock agreed. Then he said sternly, "Where did everybody go, man?"

"Stop saying everybody," said Jason.

"What?"

"Stop saying everybody. You walked from the dock to here. It's a big island."

"So where is everybody, Jason?"

"It's a big island!"

Archer said, "Let's calm down. Let's think about this."

Archer repeated to himself, *Calm down. Let's think about this.*

He couldn't get around it. The green notebooks were cataloguing nearly everything he and his friends had said and done, filled in with narration. Like somebody was watching them. Like somebody was spying. Someone was in the house. Someone was on the ferry. Someone who somehow could track their every movement and record their every word.

But they hadn't seen anybody.

Then Archer had an idea: What if this was some kind of elaborate prank? What if one of the others was manipulating this entire thing? *No, that couldn't be it. Bradley was too dumb. Tim was too distracted. Only Jason could have done this,* he thought, before dismissing the idea. *Jason would never think of this.*

Or maybe it was something else. Perhaps they were trapped in some kind of elaborate virtual reality simulation. It seemed far-fetched, but Archer was running out of theories. And when you run out of theories, the only one that explains everything— no matter how ludicrous—had to be the answer, or closest to it.

He flipped back to the start of the notebook and read the words that just moments before he could not decipher:

The four boys went camping in the state park on the mainland the weekend after their high school graduation, eating fire-cooked meals and playing cards and goofing off, assuming the entire time that the town of Echo Island would still be there when they returned.

No way, he thought.

He closed that notebook and grabbed the third, opening it to the last page. The last paragraph read:

Something occurred to him while on this trek, albeit briefly. If a sudden, say, rapture-like event had vanished everyone, why didn't anything on the island seem interrupted? Sure, traffic would be sparse on a Sunday morning, but the sudden and surprise interruption of life might have left a crashed car here and there. There'd be litter in the streets, food left out on tables uneaten. Even if the event had caused no structural or environmental damage, it would have at least left signs of life interrupted. The island looked the same as it always had, but the actual signs of life, of activity, were gone *with the inhabitants. It was like a stage set for a play that hadn't begun.*

It was a reset, he thought.

Archer's jaw dropped. Those were the last words in the notebook. And that two-word phrase jarred him: *he thought.* Now he wished he'd grabbed more of the books off the shelf. But the revelation was nearly too much.

How did they know what I was thinking?

"We are in someone's imagination." Beatrice said it, not quite asking, just repeating the statement to examine it. Then she asked, "Whose imagination?"

"There is only so much I can tell," Jack said.

Jason nearly fell, stumbling back onto the hearth, and put his head in his hands.

"Are you saying," said Beatrice, "that this is all a dream?"

"That is one way of seeing it, but the important thing is that it is not your dream."

Bradley growled. "Look, dude. Just talk to us straight."

Once again Jack seemed to look into the air, at no one in particular, and said quietly as if to himself, "It is getting quite tedious, isn't it? How long does this banter go on? I'm in this blasted place and stalling now. It's time, I think." He looked down again, this time straight to Beatrice.

"Whose dream is it?" she asked.

"Not a dream, exactly," he said. "A story."

Jason lifted his face.

"Yes," Jack said. "You are the characters in a story."

13

RUNNING

Archer had run all the way back to the cabin in the dark, only tripping twice. Without bothering to knock, he'd barged back into the room, discovering a now-roaring fire illuminating the scene much as he'd left it, with Jason and Bradley talking with Beatrice and Jack. They were in mid-conversation, but he felt no compunction about interrupting with his declaration: "Someone is watching us!"

Bradley said, "Say what now, Archway?"

"I have proof! These notebooks. Someone is recording every last thing we say. Everything we think. There is widespread surveillance, probably involving levels of artificial intelligence up to this point unknown. I think we're in the middle of a giant experiment. Government, maybe. I don't know. Maybe something more mind-boggling than that. Upper-echelon type stuff. The money and technology it would take to pull off something like this is widescale. I've been able to break the code in the notebooks, only, it's not a code exactly. It's a language, I think. And somehow, I could finally read it. I know, I haven't got it all figured out. But these things are records of everything we've said and done."

Jason looked at Jack, who was sitting silently in his desk chair and now fiddling with a pipe he'd removed from a drawer. "Everything we've done is written in there?" he asked Archer.

"Yes. It's the strangest thing."

Then, to Jack, Jason said, "What are the notebooks?"

"The notebooks are a record, just as your friend suspects. But not in the way he suspects. The notebooks keep the story alive."

"Wait. What is he talking about?" said Archer.

Beatrice spoke up then: "He says we're in a story."

Archer stopped, rolling his eyes upward, calculating. Then he said, "That's the dumbest thing I've ever heard."

"Dumber than a government simulation experiment?" Bradley said.

"Who wrote the notebooks?" Beatrice asked.

"I write them," said Jack. "What the Author gives me, I write down. It all goes onto the pages, and in the end, the whole story will be there—at least, up to the point he's done telling it."

"But the language," Jason said.

"It is a tongue from another world. There is not much I can say about that. It is a mystery the Author has not revealed."

Archer said, "You're saying we're in a story. Like, someone's imagination? Someone's *writing* this?"

"Exactly."

"Who's writing it?"

"I cannot tell you his name. I only know he is the Author."

"You can't tell us, or you don't know?"

"Both, I suppose."

Beatrice asked, "Are you the Author?"

"No. I was an author in my time, in my world. Here, I am just a guide. As others served my purposes there, here I serve his."

"So he speaks to you," Beatrice said.

"In a way."

"Wait, wait," said Archer. "You're saying *we*"—he gestured broadly at Jason, Bradley, and himself—"are in a story."

"Precisely."

"I think he means like a metaphorical story," Jason said. "As in the story of life or whatever. Telling a story with our lives."

"No," said Jack. "You are characters in a novel."

"I don't understand," said Bradley.

"No, I don't suppose you do," said Jack. "But you will. In time."

"This is insane," said Archer. "I'm not a character in a novel. I'm standing right here, in front of you."

"Both realities can be true."

"I don't think so," Archer said. "If we're characters in a novel . . . are we not real?"

"The question is strange. Do you think? Speak? Act?"

"Yes."

"Then what do you think?"

"But we're characters in a story," Archer replied. "You said that. That means we're not real."

"The one does not necessarily entail the other."

"But you're saying this whole world is made up. So it must not be real."

"I'm saying that the world in which this story is being written is more real than yours. But there is another world even more real than that one."

Archer groaned. "You're not making sense!" Then he was struck by an idea. "Oh, okay. I know what, then. If we are characters in a story, then let's have a look at the end of the story. Find out what happens next."

He bolted in front of Jack, almost bumping him out of his chair, and made for the bottom shelf of the bookcase. Pulling the last green notebook from the shelf, he opened it up to the last page. It took him a second to find the familiar strain, but the otherworldly tongue gave up its text shortly. He read:

Pulling the last green notebook from the shelf, he opened it up to the last page. It took him a second to find the familiar strain, but the otherworldly tongue gave up its text shortly. He read:

Archer shook his head, moaned. He stared back down at the page again and read:

Archer shook his head, moaned. He stared back down at the page again and read:

He slammed the notebook onto the floor.

"The words keep changing! They keep recording exactly what I'm doing in the moment, but nothing afterward!"

"You cannot read into your future," Jack said, puffing on his pipe. "That is, I'm afraid, a limitation even I share with you. He tells me what I need to know to help you. But none of us can know what will happen on each next page."

"So, we died," Jason said, "and became characters in a story? That's our fate?"

"No, no," said Jack. "The story began before you died. You've been in the story all along. Entering this underworld is just part of your story."

"So . . ." Jason wasn't sure he wanted to finish his thought. But he did. "Our families, our memories . . . none of that was real?"

"They are as real as you are, my boy."

It was too much for Archer. He was too used to figuring things out, stretching the limits of his intellect to encompass more information and adjust to new knowledge. But this? It was like trying to catch an ocean wave in a water glass.

"I—I—I . . . refuse!" he said.

Bradley straightened up. "What does that mean? You refuse what?"

"I just refuse," said Archer. He retrieved the green notebook from the floor and hurled it into the fireplace. The notebook landed in a burst of ash and a flurry of tiny red sparks.

"Archer!" Bradley said. "Relax."

"No way. I refuse to submit to this violation of . . . whatever. My will, my independence. I refuse to believe I am a character in someone else's story. Tell me it's an alternate dimension, some portal into hyperdimensionality. As far-fetched as that is, it has a grounding in natural facts. In science. This? This is stupid. It's superstition. This isn't happening."

Jack sighed. Rising from his chair, pipe clenched in his teeth, he walked over to the fireplace and pulled the notebook from the flames. It was dingy from soot but did not appear to be burned at all. He laid it down on top of the desk.

Archer willed himself not to wonder at this.

"You can all believe whatever you want to believe," Archer said. "I'm not playing this game." And he grabbed the notebook again, this time tucking it under his arm before darting for the doorway.

"Archer, stop!" Bradley called after him. "You just got here. It's dark, man."

Archer ignored him.

"And Tereus is still out there," Bradley continued.

But Archer kept walking until he was gone, slamming the door behind him.

"It's amazing that someone who can know so much can believe so little," Jack said.

"He's going to get killed," said Bradley. To Jason, he said, "Do something."

"What? Why me?"

"You're his friend. He listens to you."

"Archer doesn't listen to anybody." Jack settled back into his chair. "And that may be his undoing."

Beatrice stepped forward. "Jack. Where is this going? Are we really in a story?"

"Yes, my dear."

"Is it a good story?"

"It is."

Jason interrupted. "How can you say that? If what you're saying is true, if someone is writing all of this, then he took everything from me: my mom, my dad, my brother. Everything. He even took Tim. If someone's making this story up, he sure does take some sick pleasure in putting us through all of this. You call that *good*?"

"Not at all, lad. Bad things are bad things, whether in this world or the other. By *good*, however, I don't mean fun, entertaining, or easy. I mean good in the truest sense of the word. Even hard things can be good."

"I think I know what you mean," said Beatrice.

"Oh, brother," said Jason. "You're buying this? This isn't one of your books, Beatrice. Some silly adventure story to pass the time. If what he's saying is true, our lives are ruined."

"I don't feel that way," Beatrice said.

"Of course you don't. Your life was terrible before. You didn't lose anything you cared about."

She looked at him and radiated fury. "You have no idea what I've lost. You have no idea what I've been through. You think you've lost a family. Well, I never had one. You don't get to lecture me on what's been lost." And then her anger turned to immense grief, overwhelming her eyes with a flood cascading down her cheeks.

Jason could say nothing.

Her sorrow stared him down, withered him. He shrunk back to the hearth and put his back against the fire.

"Oh man," Bradley moaned. "I just realized something."

Beatrice looked sadly at him. "Do you want to run away like Archer?"

"What? No. I just . . . man. Everyone's going to hate me."

Beatrice had Jack's handkerchief in her hand again, and she was rubbing her nose with it. "What are you talking about?" she sniffed.

"Like, we're characters in a story, yeah? So, somebody is reading this?" He looked at Jack. "Is somebody reading this?"

Jack smiled. "Yes. At this very moment, someone is reading this."

"Good grief," Bradley said. "They're going to hate me. I'm, like, a terrible person."

"We are," Beatrice said, "who we've been written to be. That's what you're saying?"

"Yeah," Bradley said, broken about the prospect of his perception. "And I'm like the jerk guy or whatever."

"Maybe up until now. But the story's not over," Beatrice said.

"A fair, saintly Lady called to me," Jack said, "In such wise, I besought her to command me."[1]

"Huh?" Bradley said.

"She is wiser than even she knows."

"They're gonna see all of us," Bradley said. "Like, Jason's the good guy, right? And Archer's the smart one? Tim was the weak one. Beatrice is the wise one. And who am I? I'm the dumb jerk. The meathead. The guy everyone hates. And there's no changing who we are."

"Is that what you think?" Jack asked.

"That's how it always is."

Jason interjected from the fireplace, "You can't be buying into all of this."

"Quiet, bro," Bradley said. "I wanna know . . ." He was looking at Jack now with utter seriousness, with desperation. He had never felt needier, more dependent, and more vulnerable than he did now. "Can I change?"

Jack returned his gaze with the utmost tenderness. "My boy, the question is: Do you *want* to?"

"Yes. But if this is a story, I have to do what's written, right?"

"That is exactly right. And if you *want* to change, you can be sure the Author has written that too. He has written the desire into you."

"Why would he do that?"

"Regardless of what the reader thinks, maybe *the Author* likes you."

Bradley pondered this.

"Perhaps," Jack continued, "he means something by your not wanting to change before, becoming a wanting to change now."

"Come again?"

"If you want to change," Jack said, "then do."

"But what's the point?" said Jason. "Whatever we do or don't do, it's all controlled. There's an Author out there, right?"

"Yes," said Jack.

"So, I can't do whatever he's not writing. And whatever he writes, I have to do."

"That is a way of looking at it."

"No, it's not a way of looking at it. That's what it is! If we're characters in a novel, we can't do anything he doesn't write for us to do. We can't think or feel or act other than what he's writing for us. You can't deny that."

"I won't deny that."

"Maybe it would help if we knew more about the Author," Beatrice said.

"A sensible request," said Jack.

"Is he God?"

"Certainly not. He is a person, and he is the Author. But he's not God."

"Is there a God?"

"Yes, of course."

"So, the Author is not God. Is he good?"

"How do you mean?" Jack asked.

"Is he a good *writer*?"

"Ah. He's not terrible. To tell you the truth, the story is better than the writing."

"I would hate to be in a story told poorly."

"It's not as bad as all that. He's doing nearly the best he can."

"Is he a good person?" Beatrice asked.

"That's a difficult question," said Jack. "I shall say that he means you good in the end."

"That's enough for me," she said.

"This is all a mirage," said Jason.

"A story within a story," she whispered in awe.

Jason stood. "Maybe what you're saying is true. But I don't have to like it. I think Archer has the right idea. I refuse to be part of whatever story this Author wants to tell."

"But," Jack said, "the story here is not finished."

Jason placed his hands on the armrests of the chair and leaned down to look into Jack's face.

"Yes, it is," Jason said. And then he walked out of the door and into the night.

Beatrice turned to Jack. "Will he come back?"

"I am sure," Jack said. "With some coaxing."

"How is it going to end?" Beatrice asked. She was rubbing her eyes.

"I don't know," Jack said. "You will have to find out."

"What do we have to do?" said Bradley.

"Think of your favorite stories."

"I don't really read," Bradley admitted.

"I do," Beatrice said.

"And your favorite story, young lady?"

"It's called *The Green Notebook*."

"And what happens in *The Green Notebook*?"

"Oh, lots of things. But mainly, the demigod Meleager goes on adventures. He's trying to win the favor of the village and turn away the wrath of his father. There are lots of battles."

Bradley perked up. "Tereus," he said.

Beatrice had been smiling but she stopped.

"We have to . . . do what?" Bradley asked. "Fight him?"

"I never want to see him again," she said.

The image of Tereus's hulking figure emerging from the doorway of flames rushed back into Bradley's mind. He had barely survived their first encounter. Tim did not, proving that even if they were dead in the story, they could die again. And what then? What came next?

"If I go to fight him," he said, "will I win?"

"I don't know," said Jack.

"What do you mean you don't know?"

"I don't know that part of the story. The Author has not revealed it to me."

"Let's just stay here," Beatrice said. "We can be safe here."

"You are safe here," said Jack. "You would be safe in many places. But safe is not the point. Safe does not make for a good story."

14

THE CAVE

Bradley left the cabin, leaving Beatrice and Jack alone. He was not sure of anything, not anymore. But he knew he did not want to finish his story line the way he'd begun it. People were watching. It changed everything. There was accountability in that. When he and his own mind, his own feelings, were all that existed in the world, were all that mattered, it made little difference to him how he spoke or how he treated others. But the watching changed him.

Walking through the blackness of Echo Island toward some inexorable destiny, he thought of the stormy night when he'd ventured out into the ocean in the kayak, looking for the mainland. He felt so alone and yet so sure of himself.

But no more. Someone was writing. More importantly, someone was watching. Bradley felt really seen. Not simply observed, not simply considered. *Seen.*

He didn't have the intellectual capacity of Archer or the emotional reservoir of Jason, but he knew, if it were at all possible, he wanted to be different now.

This is why he was walking toward the house at Minuai Fields. The whole thing had probably burned to the ground by now, but intending again to face off with Tereus, he didn't know where else to begin.

Bradley was cutting through the Royal Garden subdivision, walking quickly but cautiously down the sidewalks. There were no lights, no noise, not even a breeze in the trees.

As he emerged on the back side of the subdivision, Bradley backed against the long row of fencing that bordered an open field. Across the expanse sat a short row of four homes. He froze. A light illuminated an upstairs window, a pale glow flickering faintly against the interior walls. A lamp, obviously. It was Archer's house.

Maybe there were more people out there. More characters. Maybe it was Tereus. Or maybe, hopefully, Archer was inside.

Bradley crossed the field and crept through the backyard. He stood directly beneath the window for a moment, considering his next move. There was likely no sneaking in.

He circled the house, peering into every window, trying to see over the stacks and stacks of books.

Checking the front door, he found it open and entered. He called out, not exactly yelling, "Archer."

No answer.

He slowly climbed the stairs and rounded the landing at the top. He could see the lamp's glow emanating from an open door to his left. Stepping through the frame, he discovered Archer there on the floor, cross-legged, the green notebook was open in his lap. Bradley let out a sigh of relief at the sight of his friend and smiled.

"It just keeps changing," Archer said.

"What does?"

"The book. I thought he had to write it. But it just keeps changing. I lose sight of what came before, like it's slipping out of my mind. I can read it one second and then, the next, I can't. But the last few lines, I can always read those, and they just keep changing."

"What do they say?" Bradley asked, taking a seat next to him.

"I've read about you walking across through Jason's neighborhood. I read about you walking up the stairs. I am reading what I'm saying right now."

"Pretty crazy."

"Pretty crazy."

"That's what I said."

"I know. I was just reading it."

"Archer, you need to close that book, man. You're going to drive *yourself* crazy if you keep staring at it."

"I just keep thinking I might see something, you know? Slightly ahead. Like there might be a jump. There's got to be stuff written after this. If we're in a book, and somebody's reading it, that means it's finished. So there's more written. I keep hoping I might get a glimpse of what comes next."

"Jack said that couldn't happen."

"He also said he was the one writing this stuff down, but here I am, staring at this thing, and it's changing without him. If he lied about that, maybe he's lying about not seeing into the next page."

"I don't know about any of that. But while you're nerding out on this stuff, we've got a killer out there. We could use your help."

Archer looked up at him for the first time. He blinked rapidly, then squinted, adjusting to see Bradley clearly. "What exactly do you think I can do?"

"Like, use your brain and stuff, man. You haven't seen this guy. He's the size of a house. He already killed Tim, and he's looking for us. And judging by how I left him, I'm guessing he's pretty torqued."

"I don't know anything about fighting."

"Dude, you can't just sit here forever. At some point, you have to do something. Even if you don't understand it all."

"Maybe that's good enough for you," Archer said. "But it's not for me." Then he buried his pointed nose back in the notebook.

With a sigh, Bradley sat on the couch. He could wait a few more minutes. He did not want to face Tereus alone.

Jason was trekking east along the wooded coastline. He followed the narrow stretch of brushless cliffs, barely caring about the treacherous path. The way was stony, dark, and, in many places, a perilous height from the rocky shore below.

At last, Jason came to the trailhead of the path down to the shore. Before stepping down, he looked out at the sea, dark and infinite under the light of a splintered moon. The water looked calm, almost like glass. There was no wind. Everything was still.

Then he heard it. That low, moaning roar. It seemed to descend from all around him, from every direction. It lasted only a few seconds, but it was more unnerving than it had been previously. The darkness had something to do with that. His solitude didn't help either.

No, no, he thought. *No more mysteries. That's not my problem anymore.*

He stepped out and down onto the narrow ledge below the trailhead and began his descent down the face of the cliff.

Carefully he stepped lower and lower, sure of each purchase, his foot against a rock or root before bringing his next foot down. His caution struck him as strange. What could he control anyway, if someone else was completely in control of his destiny? What did it matter? What if he just . . . jumped?

But he didn't. Lower and lower he climbed, keeping his balance, leaning back against the cliff, pressing his hand against the mossy ground at his back to keep himself upright until finally, he reached the bottom. Teetering across the large stones at the base of the cliff, he could see the water was lapping closer and closer. The cave was not far.

When he found it, he stared into the massive maw of darkness. Did it run all the way under the island like Beatrice had said? He could walk or crawl all the way in, deeper and deeper, until he reached the center of the known world. He could die there. It would be over.

He looked back over the ocean, the great expanse and murky depths stretching out from his feet into eternity. There was no mainland anymore. Was *anything* out there anymore?

He felt inconsolably small.

And then afraid. With the mouth of the cave at his back, its deep uncertainty open, like the mouth of a great beast swimming up to swallow him whole, he shuddered and turned back to face it.

Then, slowly, he walked into the gaping maw. But not too far. Just as far as he'd ever gone, just inside the dank and stony walls. He sat down on crossed legs with his back against the rock and closed his eyes.

He could accept his apathy. He could sit there forever. If he did nothing, said nothing, the apathy would ooze out of him and infect the whole frustrating world. He could put a wrench in the gears and end it all. Nobody would want to read a story where nothing happens.

"Jason and Archer just ran away." Beatrice was sitting on the hearth, half facing the fire, half looking at Jack, who was comfortably puffing on his pipe. "It seems like they're always running back and forth. They don't stop to think."

"It's not thinking those boys lack," Jack said. "Not all of them, anyway."

"What then?"

"They lack wonder, my dear. None of them truly wonder. Not like you."

"Wonder about what?"

"Not about. *At.* They don't wonder *at* anything. It comes, at least partly, from not reading books."

"I think Archer reads books."

"He doesn't read them," Jack said. "He uses them."

"What's the difference?"

"It's the difference between always learning but never coming to the truth."

Beatrice stretched her arms out, putting her palms to the warmth of the fire, and thought about that.

"You run too, you know," Jack finally said. "But how is your running different from theirs?"

She really thought about that. Finally, she answered: "I was running *to* the adventure, not away from it. You know?"

"I suppose you're right."

"Anyways, I'm not running now. I want to know more."

"Then I am at your service."

"I think I'm a pretty neat character," she said.

"Is that so?"

"Yes. I'm the girl. In my favorite kind of stories, the girl is always important."

"In the best stories, yes."

"And I'm not running now. I think it matters to know," she said, and she paused, folding her hands in the white pool of dress in her lap.

"To know what?"

"What kind of story we're in."

"Now you have turned a most consequential corner," Jack said, and he was beaming.

"Have you read a story like this?"

"I have written stories like this. Visitations to other worlds. Even to the underworld. They were vehicles, really, supposals— ways of exploring the transcendence under the surface of the world of the reader or around the corner from him."

"The real world."

"The *realer* world," he said.

"I've been thinking . . ."

"Wondering."

"Yes, wondering. I've been wondering about—*at*, I mean— this place, Echo Island. The names, the places. Even the premise. If we have died, then this place *is* the underworld."

"And what have you surmised?"

"It reminds me of *The Green Notebook*."

"How so?"

"The story Hippodamia was telling Ilione about Meleager. It was basically a myth."

"Gleams of celestial strength and beauty," Jack said, "falling on a jungle of filth and imbecility."[2]

"And I imagine," Beatrice said, "that knowing what kind of story we're in should help us know what to do."

"Which is what?" Jack said.

"I don't know, exactly. But I think mainly to trust the Author. And to follow his rules."

"Ah, yes! There are rules to myth. Constraints. But, at the same time, liberties."

Beatrice looked at him, eyes wide open as if she just realized something. "Is there a way out of the underworld?" she asked.

Jack replied, "Only one."

"You're just giving up, man. You're giving up." Bradley was now on the floor with Archer. "You can't do that."

"There's nothing out there anymore," Archer said. "You saw it yourself. I've been all over this island. I've done all the research I could. It's beyond me."

"Yeah. And?"

"If there's an answer, it's in here, in this notebook."

"You're just gonna sit there and keep hitting your head against a wall, man. If you want to find out what happens next, you have to get up and make it happen. Do something."

"I can't," Archer said.

Bradley grabbed him by the shoulders and shook him and growled.

Archer jerked away, terrified. "Leave me alone, Bradley. Just leave me alone."

"I'm trying to help you. You've got to get up."

"Or what? You're going to trash me? Like you've always wanted?"

Bradley *did* feel like hitting him. He always felt like hitting Archer. But for the first time ever, he felt bad about the feeling. "No," he said. "I'm not gonna do that."

Archer slumped over. He looked down at the notebook, which had skittered off his lap onto the floor.

"Look," Bradley said. "The whole thing kind of freaks me out too. I don't understand it all, but we can't let that stop us from doing something. I mean, Tereus killed Tim. We can't get him back. And Tereus will keep going until he's through with all of us. And I don't want to lose anyone else."

Archer said nothing.

"I'm going to leave you here," Bradley said. "And you just remember it was your choice." He stood up, brushing his pants off. "And clean your house, man. It's gross."

He left then and continued his journey across the vacant lot toward the town center and, beyond it, Minuai Fields.

Passing the Bee Market, he thought of Tim, how he couldn't protect him, how his record of simultaneously sticking up for him and ensuring the role of tormenting Tim was his alone, had been broken. He wondered what had happened to him, what happens *after*. They were dead. But they could die again. And then what?

Crossing the street by the newspaper machine he'd destroyed what seemed like ages ago, Bradley stopped to consider it. A sudden jolt of pleasure shot through his body as he recalled stomping the plexiglass cover open.

And then the darkness seemed to grow darker. He looked up.

"Where's my daughter?"

Tereus was walking up the sidewalk toward him with purpose. His face was difficult to discern in the soft moonlight. But as he came closer, Bradley noticed that the skin on his face, arms, and hands was sloughed, peeling off, bubbled, and raw—no doubt from the fire.

Bradley backpedaled and tripped over the newspaper box. He'd barely regained his footing when Tereus was upon him.

How long had Jason been sitting in the cave? He didn't know. It felt like hours. He thought at some point he would just disappear into nothingness, born back into the void of nonexistence, back to before the story began. But he still existed. And the rocky floor was killing his hindquarters.

He was startled by the whisper of wind on his face and opened his eyes. After days of stillness, the brush of a breeze against his cheeks felt strange, as if something was shifting. Now he could see the first rays of dawn streaming warmly into the mouth of the cave, and there in the entry, as if leading a procession of light, was Beatrice, the beatific dawn her crown. Her white dress danced in the breeze.

"Jason," she said.

He said nothing.

"What are you doing?" she asked.

He looked at her obliquely, words welling up but unspilled.

"Answer me."

He opened his mouth as if to speak but still said nothing.

"I said," she said, "what are you doing?"

He thought perhaps a final comment might be warranted. "Nothing," he said. "That's the point. If I sit here and do nothing, there can't be a story."

"You're being foolish."

"No. This whole thing is foolish. It's not fair. But as long as I can choose, I choose for there not to be a story."

"I don't think you can choose that," Beatrice said.

"Of course I can. Nothing happens next. Because I'll just sit here. Nobody's going to read a story about a guy who just sits in a cave."

"If he was interesting enough, they might."

Jason looked at her, hurt.

"You know," she said, "trying to stop a whole story like this is *kind of* interesting." She was smirking.

"This is serious," he said.

"Of course it is. And you definitely shouldn't do anything you don't want to do. But you can choose to want to do great things. And sitting in a cave forever is kind of interesting. But it's not great."

She was smiling big at him now, and he was softening, despite himself.

"What if I can overpower the Author?" Jason said. "That would be something great, wouldn't it? Anyone reading the story would want to know the answers. And if I just sit here and stop the whole thing, they won't keep reading. That's power."

"But they *would* keep reading," she said. "You couldn't stop them."

"Why?"

"Because they'd want to know what happened next! They wouldn't know that nothing happened if they didn't turn the page. They wouldn't even be sure you would sit here forever if they didn't keep reading."

No, he thought. *It's too much. I refuse.* He said, "I'm going to stop it."

"You can't. You can't control it."

"What I don't get is why you aren't angry. What's wrong with you? What you've been through. The family you were given."

"I can choose."

"But you can't. Can't you see? If what Jack said is true, you can't. I'm not even going to talk. If I do nothing, say nothing, it's over."

"Jason."

He folded his arms.

"Jason," she said again.

He looked down, ignored her, willed her to disappear, willed the whole world to disappear.

He eked out, "I could kill myself."

"You wouldn't do that."

"How do you know?"

"Because *you* want to see."

She stood with her head cocked, hand on her hip, looking compassionately at him.

In a moment, it was no longer the world that was too much. The island, the vanishing of his family, the threat of a madman on the loose thirsty for blood—all began to fade from the force of her reprimand. Even the confounding, constraining weightiness of knowing his story was being written from the outside began to feel lighter compared to the glory of her slight presence, her wisp of an arm now outstretched from a rising sun.

"Jason," she said. She was holding out her hand. "Come with me."

What was happening?

He looked at Beatrice's hand. It was a miracle. The first time she'd ever reached for him. Jason couldn't refuse.

So he took her hand. He stood up. And she led him out of the darkness and back into the story.

15

THE CHARGE

Bradley had to think fast. Sprawled on the sidewalk beside the newspaper box, he began scrambling backward as the towering shadow of the man seemed to swoop down onto him.

"Where's my daughter?" Tereus repeated, his large hand grasping at Bradley's ankle.

Bradley kicked free and launched himself upright, but Tereus closed the gap instantly, and an incredible force exploded in Bradley's gut. It was the biggest punch he'd ever taken. He was back on the sidewalk, and Tereus was not stopping. The man was standing over Bradley, whose legs were now twitching slightly against the concrete as he desperately tried to catch his breath.

Tereus reached down, grabbed hold of Bradley's shirt, and lifted him up. Bradley was not what anyone would consider small, yet the man lifted him like he was a rag doll.

And then, the adrenaline kicked in. Bradley knew if he was going to survive, he would have to fight. All his senses went electric, rapid-fire, the violence subterranean in him suddenly bursting forth through his will. He grabbed the man's wrist with his left hand and, using it as leverage, pivoted himself powerfully to the right, his right fist hurtling into Tereus's rib cage.

It happened so quickly, the man didn't have time to protect himself. It was the same side Bradley had collided into when he blind-tackled Tereus by the trailer. The man let out an "oof" as he dropped Bradley's shirt and stumbled over. But just two steps.

Then he stood back up, and he brought his fists up to fight.

Bradley jumped to his feet and prepared to do the same.

They stared at each other's faces in the dark Echo Island street for a moment, each waiting for the other to make the first move.

Tereus interrupted the stalemate with a flurry of punches that mostly landed on Bradley's arms and shoulders as he raised them to protect his head. But Tereus was quicker than he looked, and he varied his blows like a boxer, going low when Bradley protected high and vice versa. It took just seconds for Tereus to begin moving Bradley backward.

But the boy was still on his feet. And while he thought that at any moment the strike would come that broke his ribs or jaw or knocked him out, he absorbed them all, keeping his balance while inching back, and waiting for the right opening.

It came as Tereus swung his gigantic fist vertically in an uppercut at his jaw. Bradley instinctively leaned right, rather than back, which would have afforded him no leverage at all in a counterstrike. As the ramming force narrowly missed his chin, he swung himself again with all his strength to the right and hammered the man in his wounded ribs. Something definitely cracked this time.

But he'd now injured his own hand in the strike, maybe even broken a couple of his fingers.

Tereus grabbed his side, wincing. He let out a low growl.

Bradley held his right fist in his left hand and tried to will the pain away. Then he thought it would be wiser to run, especially while his opponent was distracted.

He didn't have time. Tereus was on him again, quicker and angrier than before.

At first, Bradley put up a good defense again. As the two grappled into the street, from a distance, you wouldn't know who was who. But Bradley couldn't keep up the intensity. His stronger hand was growing more useless as, fighting against the pain, he kept using it against the man who only seemed to increase in strength.

Bradley ran out of steam. Unable to throw more punches, he covered his head with his arms to protect himself. Tereus's next punch broke Bradley's right wrist, so he dropped his hands. The next punch struck Bradley in the side of the head. There was a sharp ringing sound and a bright flash in his head for just half a second before he was plunged into blackness.

Jason hovered outside the cabin door, looking sheepish and defeated, but curious.

Beatrice stood just inside the doorway in front of him, greeting Jack with abundant cheer. "I brought him back," she said.

"So I see," said Jack. Craning his neck to gaze over Beatrice's shoulder, he called out, "And where had you planned to go?"

Jason didn't reply, so Beatrice did for him. "He went to a cave on the western shore." When Jack didn't answer, she added, "He thought if he just went in there and never left, he could stop the story."

Jack chuckled.

Jason, a little irritated, stepped forward into the doorway. "I don't like the idea of not having a choice, is all. You have to understand, this is a lot to take in."

"Oh, of course," said Jack. "Wrestling with the story is part of the story. There's no getting beyond that. In a way, I admire the attempt to force your will upon the story, to control everything. Each of you has had your own version of that, I think."

"Yes," Jason said. "I can see that."

"But for every Jonah, vomited to shore from the diseased gills of his very escape, there are perhaps countless corpses bobbing about inside the bellies of fish."

"I just want to know," said Jason, "now what?"

"The story has won out in your case. At least for the moment. We must make sure it wins at every turn."

"See, I just don't know what that means."

"Dear boy, you tried to force your will upon the story. And then you found it bent, did you not, by another?" He gestured to Beatrice, who responded with a playful curtsy. "And thus, you see that there's no outrunning—or out-*sitting*, in your case, I suppose—the will of the Author. Now we must make sure that you follow the story to its projected end—that, in effect, your will aligns with the Author's."

"We want to know what to do next," said Beatrice.

"Yes," said Jack. "As I was saying to the young lady before she commenced her mission, the key to navigating any story in which you find yourself is determining what kind of story you are in."

"And what kind of story is that?" said Jason.

"Why, don't you see?" Beatrice turned to him. "We are characters in a myth."

Jason frowned. "What's a myth? Like a lie?"

"You must not see myth as corresponding primarily to something untrue," Jack said, "but quite the opposite. Myths, whether they be fictions or not, tell us extraordinarily true things, sometimes in their most elemental substance."

"I don't understand," said Jason. "Myths, by definition, are untrue. That's why we say something is a myth."

Mostly to himself, Jack said, "What *do* they teach in the schools these days?" Then he looked full upon Jason's face and added, "A myth is traditionally a fiction, yes. Something ahistorical. But for something to be a myth, in the classic sense, it must convey truth, and I would say, in fact, a much deeper truth sometimes than other kinds of fictions."

Jack paused to gauge if they were paying attention.

While Jason looked confused, Beatrice's eyes were bright. She said eagerly, "Yes, go on."

"Of course, there are the myths that turn out to be historical truths, after all. See, in the world in which your story is written, there are thousands of myths, just like there are in this world. Some of them are the same. And each of them has some bit of truth in them. But there is *one* myth that is, if you understand, a true story. A myth that is fact."

Jack and Beatrice exchanged looks.

"But I digress. Let's discuss this myth *you* are in presently. Your story is a fictional tale meant to reveal something true. To be a character in a myth is a high calling indeed."

"Why? What difference does it make to us?" Jason said. "Who cares about any of this?"

Jack straightened, became indignant. "Who cares? Why, the Author does! That's who. And so does any reader who's managed to read to this point. They want to see where it goes next, don't you see? And if you're honest with yourself, boy, you will admit that it also matters to you. *You* care. Or else you wouldn't be standing here just now."

"You mentioned rules," Beatrice said. "About myths, I mean. What are the rules?"

"It is something that men in many myths never seem to be aware of. It is why Dante gives himself Virgil. It is why the Author of this story has sent me. To guide the potential heroes along the way through their mystery. You must know a few things to manage well enough.

"As I said, myths communicate truth of some kind, and by that, I do not simply mean facts. Aside from the one myth, every other myth is a fiction. And yet, myths still tell the truth or mean to. For instance, the subservience of mankind to the gods—his inability to prevail against them, to trick them without recourse—is a reflection of the fatalism of many cultures. What truth is the Author of your story conveying? He chose to tell this kind of story for a reason."

"To toy with us," Jason said. "I mean, he began the story by causing our car to crash and bringing us to this underworld."

"Yes, but don't you see?" Jack said. "Don't you see how suddenly that put you on a different kind of adventure? One that tells a truth that surpasses even the world you once knew.

Walking through death clarifies, making what is passing less real and what is lasting more so. The choices you make here—in this place—in all ways matter more."

"But that's another thing," Jason said. "If we're already dead, why can we die in this underworld? As far as we know, Tim has died. What happens then? How can we die again?"

"It is not the first dying that ends things for all people. It is the second dying that does that. Death here is really death."

"It was dying," Beatrice offered, "that brought us all here."

"Precisely," Jack said. "That end was shared. But you will not all share the second end."

Jason wandered over to the bookcase and traced his finger along the spines of the green notebooks. "Beatrice's father. Is he going to kill us all?"

"That part has not been given to me," said Jack.

"But he wants to."

"Yes, that is my understanding. There is something insatiable in the man, and for all the robbery he has done in his life, he continues to think himself the victim. The reason he and Beatrice are here was born of his perverted sense of being owed, a sense of sovereignty, which, of course, you now know does not belong to any of us. And dying did not take that away. He still wants what he thinks is his."

Jason looked down for a moment, staring at the planks on the floor. Then he turned to look at Beatrice. One tear jeweled in the corner of her eye.

"Beatrice," Jason said.

When she looked at him, he could see the fear in her face as real and as raw as the happiness there had been just minutes before.

"Yes," Jack said. "It's Beatrice he wants. Or rather, what she represents to him. But you must remember what kind of story the Author is telling. What truth is he telling?"

"Can't you stop him?" said Jason.

"The Author? Certainly not. I am as much a character written here as you are."

"No. I mean Tereus."

"Ah. I am sorry, but that is not my role. I am the guide, not the hero."

"Wait," Jason said. He was beginning to feel crushed by the weight of the thing.

"The charge has not been given to me," Jack said.

"But I'm not a hero either," Jason said.

"Bah!" Jack said. "You've been believing that your whole life. Now is the time to act. Now is the time to wonder. Heroes arise when the time comes. What kind of story do you think you're in, dear boy? The kind where characters sit in caves and sleep their lives away?"

"I don't know."

"Well, know. *Do* know. There's a supernatural vanishing and a dramatic secret. There's an ocean, a girl, and a great villain seeking to kill you all. Does that sound like the kind of story that wouldn't have a hero?"

Jason wanted to ask if he was supposed to be the hero, but he was afraid the answer was no. And he was also afraid the answer was yes. Finally, he said, "What should I do?"

"Own your part in the story," said Jack. "After a while, it will begin to feel as though you are writing it yourself. Ask yourself, what good should happen next? Will it, and you can know it is being willed."

Jason listened, speechless.

Jack continued, "It is time to become the person that you are destined to become. There is no other way. What kind of chap do you want to be? You must face that fire. This is the charge."

When Bradley came to, he found himself tied to a tree with nautical rope, front-wise but sitting, his arms and legs pulled forward around the trunk and bound on the other side. He lifted his head away and felt the scrape of the bark on his face.

He pulled with all his might, and his shattered right hand splintered in pain against the binding. A soft yelp slipped from his mouth, and then he heard the crunch of leaves and straining of twigs beneath approaching footsteps.

There was a hot breath on his ear. "How many of you are there?"

Bradley turned his face away and planted the side of his head against the tree.

Tereus grabbed his hair on the back of his head, pulled back, and smashed his forehead against the tree trunk. Instantly, Bradley was dizzy again and on the verge of blacking out.

"I will kill you right here," Tereus said. "You think you're such a tough guy."

"I—" Bradley said, but he had to swallow. His eyes lolled and stars shot against his eyelids.

Tereus pulled his head back again and breathed on his face, "Yeah?"

"I was gonna say—" Bradley gasped.

"Go on."

"I was gonna say that I have a fever. And the only prescription is more cowbell." And then Bradley smiled through his bloody teeth.

Tereus stood up, took a step back, and then kicked Bradley in the side.

In spite of himself, Bradley began to cry from the pain, choking on his breath.

The man crouched beside him again. His charred nose was practically on Bradley's cheek. "You know, I really don't know what's happening here. I don't know where everybody went. And I don't know where you kids keep coming from. But I know somebody has my daughter. And one of you knows where she is."

He cocked his head and continued. "You are a tough guy, aren't you? Not like your friend. He was a big baby—let me tell you. But you knew that. You knew what a big, fat baby he was."

Bradley was looking at Tereus out of the corner of his eye now with a seething rage. He wished he could've pulled the whole tree down on top of him.

"You should have heard him squeal," Tereus said, "when that fire caught him."

Bradley pulled against the trunk again. The pain in his hand shot up his arm into his shoulder. He'd break everything trying to get free.

Tereus reached around the tree and grabbed Bradley's broken hand and squeezed.

The boy screamed.

The man did not let up. He kept squeezing against the shattered bones, creating new fractures, and said, "Where is she?"

"Okay! Okay!"

Tereus looked at Bradley's bloodstained and tear-streaked face. "Tough guy," he said.

"I'll tell you. I'll tell you."

"I know you will. Tell me."

"You—you go south through town, toward the ferry landing."

"Yes?"

"The woods right on the waterfront to the west of the landing."

"Yes, I know them."

"Yeah," Bradley panted. "You go to those woods, stay to the north side, *this side* of them, right? About a hundred yards along that line, you come to a really big pine tree. And when you come to that really big pine tree . . ."

"Okay."

"And then—"

"Yes?"

"And then you shove it up your butt."

Bradley started laughing to himself again.

Tereus stopped and thought a moment. Then he put his hands around Bradley's throat.

Jack sat alone in the cabin in the woods, diligently poring over a half-filled green notebook at his desk, a mournful wisp of smoke twirling up from the bowl of his pipe.

His pen was busy.

"Tongue of angels," he muttered to himself. "I can't say I understand it, but here it is. Here it all is, moving to its inexorable end."

He stopped for a moment and spoke into the air, "I'm ready for a rest, I should say," and then resumed writing, adding quickly as he did, "It's been ages since I've had a walk, you know."

Outside, the wind began to pick up. Jack could hear the low whistle of the air throttling through the cracks of the cabin and the rattle of dead leaves nicking against the glass of the window.

"Oh, is this what we're doing?"

A peal of thunder shook the roof.

The door flung open, and a rush of wind burst into the room, violently rustling the pages of the notebook under his hands. His pen fervently scribbled against them.

Rising to close the door, upon turning, Jack saw the hulking figure of Tereus filling the entryway.

"Ah," Jack said.

16

MINUAI FIELDS

What happens in *The Green Notebook*?" Jason asked.

The wind was steadily pushing against Jason and Beatrice as they made a solemn walk across the outskirts of downtown. Rain fell in fat, scattered droplets onto their skin.

"A lot of things happen," Beatrice said.

"No. I mean, like, at the end."

"Oh."

"They all live happily ever after, right?"

"Well . . . sort of. Meleager goes on all these adventures in order to win the hearts of his people. He has to, or his father will kill him."

"This is the unnamed god."

"Right."

"So Meleager promises to turn the people's favor back to his father. He defeats some of their enemies in battle. He retrieves legendary talismans they believe in. He gets rid of some horrible creatures that prey on the people at night. That kind of thing."

"And in the end? He finishes the quests and accomplishes the mission, right?"

"Yes," Beatrice said. "But there's this twist, a little thing at the end that kind of upends everything."

"What happens?"

"Meleager does finally win the acclaim of the people, who now return to honoring his father. And because of that, his father does spare him. But then . . ."

"Yeah?"

"In the end, he falls in love."

"He does?"

"Yes. And this woman, she's evil. She tests his pride, basically. She tells him it isn't fair that his father is getting all the glory when he's done all the work. She reminds him of all the places he's gone, all the enemies he's conquered, and all the times he could've died. This woman convinces him that the villagers should be honoring *him*—basically, worshiping *him*—instead of his father."

"What does he do?"

"One of the talismans he recovered from the sea is this comb said to have been used by an unnamed goddess."

"A comb?"

"Yes."

"Like, for hair?"

"Yes. Just listen for a second! So he recovers this comb, which is believed to contain supernatural powers because a goddess used it. And once upon a time, one of her hairs was found in it, and some warrior used it as his bowstring, and he never lost a battle, or something like that. The comb was put in a temple to the unnamed god, the one for Meleager's father. It's like a shrine. And this woman convinces Meleager to go steal it from the temple and from his father. Really, she wants it, because she thinks it will make her immortal. But she convinces him that he deserves to have it."

"So, he goes to steal it, I'm guessing."

"Yes. And at the end, his father strikes him dead right there in the temple."

"And?"

"And that's it."

"That's the end of the story?"

"Yeah. Well, I mean, it goes back to the slave girls at the fire, but that's the end of the part about Meleager."

They kept trudging forward, fighting against the wind. Jason bit his lip, thinking. Finally, he said, "Well, that's not inspiring at all."

The rain continued to fall in fits and starts, and thunder approached from the distance.

"I think we're about to get dumped on," Jason said. "We can cut through my neighborhood here. I want to see my house one more time."

"Don't say that," Beatrice said. "Don't say it like you'll never see it again. You don't know what's going to happen."

"I just don't have a great feeling about whatever it is I'm supposed to do. And I know this story is somehow wrapped up in *The Green Notebook*, and you just told me that Meleager dies. So, what am I supposed to think?"

"I think," Beatrice said, "that you're supposed to think that anything is possible. That's the point."

Lightning streaked across the sky, instantly followed by the boom of thunder directly overhead. The rain grew intense.

"Let's hurry," Jason said. "We're almost there."

They rushed to the house in the pouring rain, dripping everywhere upon entry, where Jason immediately tripped over something on the floor. It was too dark to identify until another flash of lightning lit up the foyer. It was a drawer yanked from its slot in the entryway cabinet, and beyond it, in that split second of white light through the windows, they could see the entire living room was a mess.

"What . . ." Jason said.

"My father."

Jason froze. Then he whispered, "Do you think he's here?"

"No, I bet not. But I'm sure he came here looking for guns. Or for me. Or both. Did your dad have a gun?"

"No. My family didn't really hunt. My dad just did every now and then with buddies. He always borrowed something from them. But—"

"What?"

Jason crept through the blackness of the living room, arms out in front of him and shuffling his feet, anticipating obstructions. As his eyes adjusted to the darkness, he reached the kitchen and could see the whole place torn apart, the floor strewn with the contents of cabinets and drawers. Including a slew of knives.

He retrieved a long chef's knife and held it up before his eyes. Then he remembered. "Oh wait," he said. "My brother."

"What about your brother?"

"He's got this ridiculous hunting knife. Like a Rambo knife."

"I don't know what that is."

"It's like a real knife with a grip. For hunting, or . . . you know, for combat."

"I thought your family didn't hunt."

"We don't, not really. Scott's just a weirdo." Jason smiled thinking about him.

Cautiously, he climbed the steps, Beatrice following behind. At the landing, he stopped, looking back to his parents' room. *Just one more look.*

The first thing he noticed was the sharp smell of perfumes in the air, acidic florals and spices stinging his nose. Beatrice said nothing as he looked over the unmade bed. This floor, too, was covered in the ransacked contents of Tereus's search. It appeared that Tereus had thrown everything from their closet onto the carpet, and the bathroom looked like a grenade had gone off. All of his mother's perfumes and cosmetic potions had been swept from their glass shelf, some of them now lay on the floor, others, in cracked vials on the counter beneath the shattered mirror.

Jason felt suddenly protective of his family. His home had been violated. His parents' things destroyed. A lightning bolt of rage cracked through his nerves. And he wasn't sure whom he was really angry with. Tereus? Or someone else?

Jason walked out and across the landing toward his brother's room.

"It smells bad in here," Beatrice said.

"Yeah," he said, and he smiled. It meant his brother was real.

On his hands and knees beside the bed, he reached under the box spring and felt around under the slats. "Scott kept it under here, hidden between the mattress and the frame because my mom told him to get rid of it."

After a few seconds, Jason found it. It was long and olive green, the blade serrated on one side, and the hilt grooved for maximum grip. It was the kind of novelty knife you might find for sale at a flea market or a gas station. Real hunters would not have used it. But it was big and sharp, and it made him feel a bit calmer, sensing what lay ahead.

"I'm going to change," Jason said. "My room's right there. Do you want to see if you can find something in my parents' room? Your dress is soaked."

Indeed, it was. Beatrice simply nodded, returning to the master bedroom to search in the darkness for something of his mother's.

Jason changed into dry jeans, a long-sleeved athletic shirt, and his water-resistant windbreaker. He didn't notice what Beatrice had put on until they'd returned to the front porch to exit. It was a powder blue dress, plain and unpatterned, rather similar to her white one in style—with thin straps over her bare shoulders and a hem to her knees. Jason had never seen it before.

The rain was falling now in a loud, unrelenting cascade, and water was pooling along the curbs.

"Don't you think that's a little . . ."

"What?" she said.

He wanted to say *impractical*. Did she really think that was a great outfit for being outside in a rainstorm? Or for whatever it was they were about to walk into?

Instead, he just said, "Hold on." He opened the hall closet to rummage around, emerging with a long gray raincoat. "At least wear this so that you don't get cold and drenched."

He moved to help her into it, but she said, "I can do it," and took it from him to put it on herself.

Jason looked out the window. "I guess there's no avoiding this."

"No. I think it's part of the thing," she said. "The story."

Jason let out a big, heavy sigh. Then he stepped out into the rain—Beatrice right beside him—and began his journey to Minuai Fields.

Jack leaned forward in his chair as if to welcome the bad man in. His brow was arched. A new fire was blazing in the fireplace, but the pleasant crackling of wood was drowned out by the rain beating on the roof.

Tereus assessed the scene, scanning the room furtively. He was nearly snorting, out of breath but churning with fury. It felt like a trap, though he couldn't see how. Certainly, the chubby bald man in the corner posed no threat. And there was no place for anyone to hide, really. So he stepped in and slammed the door behind him.

"Manners," Jack said.

Tereus snarled.

Jack leaned back. "Come in, then. I've been expecting you."

The man closed the gap between Jack and himself with what seemed to Jack like supernatural quickness. One moment, he wasn't beside him, and the next, his fists were on the desk and he was pushing his melted face into Jack's, seething with anger and dripping water into his lap.

Through the remnants of his singed beard, he said, "Where is my daughter?"

"It's remarkable," said Jack. "You are a formidable adversary; there's no doubt of that. But terribly banal."

Tereus didn't know what that meant, but he knew it wasn't a compliment. He wrapped his fingers around Jack's neck and squeezed, or tried to. He suddenly found his muscles unresponsive.

"You cannot harm me," said Jack. "That much I've been told."

The signals were sending, but they weren't being received. In his mind, Tereus was choking the old man—his eyes bulging out, his tongue lolling, and his already-red face turning crimson. But in reality, nothing was happening. His hand would not obey orders.

"Try and try. It won't work. I've been assured."

Tereus dropped his hand, then lifted it before his eyes, dumbly.

"I only wish," Jack said, "I could pass it on to the children. But I suppose it wouldn't make much of a story if no one could get hurt."

"Who are you?" Tereus said.

"My name is Jack, though any information beyond that I don't think should matter much to you. But you are to have a seat. That much I know. I don't know that it is supposed to do any good, but I'm to have a talk with you."

"I want to know where my daughter is."

"In due time. For now, I insist. Sit down."

Jack motioned at the fireplace. Tereus stared at the hearth for a moment and then, stunningly, complied, turning to place his enormous haunches on the brick. He entirely blocked the fireplace from view.

"I am meant," Jack said, "to prevail upon you to turn from your path. I do not expect you to comply. But I must make the plea."

"I don't understand," said Tereus. He looked like a gigantic child huddled over his own knees. Seated a full foot below Jack's chair and slumped, his head was still level with the guide's.

"And I don't suspect you will. Nevertheless, I am to make the appeal. And there it is: Cease from your current path. Cease all anger, hatred, and violence."

Tereus perked up. The corner of his lip curled.

"And," Jack continued, "you must renounce your claim upon Beatrice."

At that, Tereus shot up and bolted toward Jack. But again, he ran up against some invisible force, which buffeted him back. He could not even touch the man.

Jack sighed. "Sit down, you fool," he said calmly.

Tereus pressed against the invisible wall, which wouldn't give. He reared back and rammed his shoulder against it. "You've trapped me!"

"No, you scourge. You've trapped yourself. You are free to leave and carry on your path of destruction, which will inevitably lead to your own, whether in this story or the next. But I haven't yet pleaded with you properly. It is my next assignment and the next thing that must happen. So, please. Sit down."

Reluctantly, Tereus complied, once again hunching on the brick lip of the fireplace. This time, however, he fixed his demonic gaze on Jack, waiting for any sign that the barrier might be down. He said, "I just want my daughter."

"I know. But Beatrice is beyond you now. She always has been. Her innocence, her purity, her hope. Heavens! Her imagination. With all your strength, with all your rage, you could not keep her from her destiny. Nor yourself from yours. The fate of the boys I cannot see. You may indeed succeed in your bloodlust there. Something tells me it may be that sort of myth. But not so with Beatrice. I suspect, however the rest of it turns out, that Beatrice has already escaped for good."

"Stop saying her name!"

"A name given by her mother, I think."

"Stop."

"Do you agree, then? You will renounce your violence against the boys and give up your claim on the girl?"

Tereus stood again, slowly this time. The notebooks had caught his eye.

Jack said, "That's a no, then?"

Ignoring him, Tereus crossed to the bookcase. He pulled one of the green notebooks from the shelf and opened it.

Jack said, "Don't bother yourself with those. They are undoubtedly beyond you."

Tereus frowned sideways at him but kept the pages open before him.

"I'm saying," Jack insisted, "you cannot hope to read what is there."

The man now looked fully at Jack. "I can read it just fine," he said.

"How's that?"

Tereus began reading, slowly: "Tim was back at the Bee Market again, shopping. He wheeled a squeaking grocery cart brimming with bags of chips and boxes of cereal up and down the Bee Market aisles, wistfully eyeing each row. The comforting sights of colorful logos and perfectly photographed meals on package after package drew him steadily along. Food made him absentminded."

Jack sat up straight. "Fascinating."

"Tim had just reached the end of the baking goods aisle when he heard it," Tereus continued. "A clanging sound from outside."

"Well, this is a development I didn't see coming."

"What does it mean?" Tereus asked.

"It means there's a great deal more I haven't been told; I'll tell you that much! Perhaps it means even the demons understand."

Tereus dropped the notebook on the floor and removed another one from the shelf. Scanning random pages, he threw that one down and chose another. Jack watched him mournfully. "And tremble."

The beast was catching on. Eventually, he chose the last notebook on the shelf and began flipping through the pages to the end. After long seconds that felt to Jack like long minutes, Tereus dropped that notebook too. "Minuai Fields," he said.

"What's that?"

"They've gone to Minuai Fields."

"Yes, that sounds right."

"And what happens next?"

"I do not know, exactly. It hasn't been given to me, though I suspect, in one sense, it's already been written."

"Minuai Fields. Then what?"

"As I said, I cannot say. It was only for me to implore you to turn back, knowing that despite the warning, you would continue. Not even you can defeat the story itself. But the story's end is coming soon, and I trust yours along with it."

Tereus reached out and grasped the bookcase. He pulled it toward him, spilling all the notebooks onto the floor in a great heap. "That's what I think of your story," he said.

Jack shook his head.

The bookcase fell over then, landing with a thud on top of its spillage.

"I'm going to kill them," he said.

"They are just boys," Jack said. And as Tereus retreated back out of the cabin and into the dark deluge, Jack added under his breath, "Though sometimes the battle reveals the man."

Despite the new clothes, Jason and Beatrice were both practically soaked through when they reached Minuai Fields. The great expanse of grass rose gently to meet them. It was naturally thin, wispy grass, typically delicate under their feet but now thickened in the rain. Their feet sloshed in the softening earth.

Jason looked out over the dreary field. The wind cut through it at every angle. In the distance, over the edge of the cliff on the other side, lightning illuminated the ocean.

"My dad used to bring me here to fly kites." There was silence for a moment. Then he said, "That's all I remember about this place."

Beatrice glanced up at the sky as if imagining herself as a girl flying a kite.

"Didn't you live over there?" Jason said. He was pointing across the field eastward, in the direction where the burned-out trailer still sat below a ridge, obscured by the elevation and the night.

"Yes," Beatrice said, but she didn't even look.

Something else caught her eye. "What is that?" she said.

Jason followed her gaze westward.

"In the trees," she said.

It was hard to tell in the distance and in the rain.

"Do you see it?" she said.

"Yes."

It looked like a pile of laundry against a tree. They began to slog through the ankle-high grass until they knew what they were approaching, and then they ran.

"Bradley," Jason said, horrified.

He was wet and bloody. Still tied to the tree, he looked crumpled, half of himself.

"Is he . . . ?" Beatrice said.

"Bradley!"

His swollen eyes fluttered slightly. A tiny, weak cough puffed through his split lips.

"What happened?" Jason said.

"Don't, don't," Bradley said.

"Bradley, it's us. It's me."

"Jason?"

"Yes."

"Ohhh," he moaned.

"Did he do this to you?"

"Yes. I—"

"Hold on; we're gonna get you untied."

"I'm sorry, man," Bradley said.

"Don't be stupid. We're gonna get you free, just hold on for me."

Bradley groaned. "It hurts so bad. I wish he'd killed me."

Jason withdrew his knife, and Beatrice shook her head, saying, "No, not like that," and she began untying the knots as gingerly as she could. It was hard work. Twice she pushed too hard on Bradley's right hand, and he grimaced in pain.

Eventually his legs and wrists were free, and he fell on his back on the wet ground. He opened his mouth to taste the rain.

After a while, Jason said, "Do you think you can stand?"

"Yeah. Not yet, but yes. Give me a sec, okay?"

The three of them huddled there in the trees for several minutes. The weather was biting, but Jason almost wished it could last forever. He had not forgotten why they were there.

Finally Bradley said, "I told him about the cabin. I can't believe it. I thought maybe you were there. I thought maybe he might have . . ."

"It's okay," said Jason. "You had to. I mean, I think it was what needed to happen next for some reason. Before this."

"What are you guys doing here?"

"I don't know. I just knew that this is where I was supposed to come. I think I'm supposed to wait for him," Jason said.

"Wait. What? He's coming back here?"

"I think so."

"You don't want to mess with this guy, man. Look at me. He did . . . he really hurt me, man."

"I know. But I don't think there's any avoiding it now. We have to go through it. I thought for a while that we could get out. But I don't think it's possible."

"Jason, look," Bradley said.

"What?"

"I . . . I can't fight him. I'm in no shape."

"I know. Bradley, it's okay. You're not supposed to. It's supposed to be me."

Bradley seemed to consider that. Jason assumed he was thinking the situation was totally hopeless now.

Finally, Bradley said, "What's your plan?"

"Plan? I don't know. I mean, I have a knife."

Bradley started laughing, which quickly turned to a sputter of coughs.

"What's so funny?" Jason said.

"You know what?" Bradley said through gritted teeth. "Jason, man, I'm glad we're friends."

"Yeah," Jason said. "I guess I am too."

"Dude, I tried with Archer. I tried to convince him, to get him to come with me."

"I know. It's okay. We'll get him later. He's safe right now."

"No, I don't think so," Bradley said. "He didn't seem right. But I'll tell you . . ." He coughed, and a bit of blood spit from his mouth. "I keep hoping some tank will come rolling over the hill, and that Archer made it work. Wouldn't that be something?"

"If anyone could do that," Jason agreed, "Archer could."

Beatrice broke in to say, "It feels like a dream, doesn't it?"

"Not to me," said Bradley. He was holding his stomach as a fresh wave of pain rumbled through.

"I know it's real," she said. "But there's something more real out there, I'm sure of it. It can't all be gone. We can find another place, another world. We can do that, don't you think?"

Neither of the boys said anything. Neither of them was sure.

Thunder cracked overhead, and suddenly, there came a voice bellowing, "Beatrice!"

She shuddered.

Jason wheeled around, scanned the horizon. He began to shake too.

"What—what's happening?" Bradley said.

"Shhh," Jason said.

Rolling over the field, thunderous as the sky, came the call again. "Beeeatrice!"

"Is that him?" said Bradley.

"Be quiet a second; I need to think."

With his good hand, Bradley grabbed him by the windbreaker sleeve and whispered, "Jason, Jason."

"What, man?"

"He's hurt. On his left side. Ribs. I hurt him."

"Okay, okay," Jason said. He turned slowly away, and Bradley grabbed him again.

"Jason."

"What?" Jason said, and he was looking around nervously as if Tereus might be upon them any second now.

Bradley pulled him down close to his face. "Hey, man. Look at me."

"Yeah, Bradley, what?"

He waited until Jason had locked eyes with him, and he said, "Don't die, dude."

Jason stopped. He smiled, but just for a second. Then he shook free of Bradley's grip and sat upright.

I don't think I can do this.

He turned to tell Beatrice. "I don't think—"

But she wasn't there.

He stood up then and could see in the near distance, his mother's raincoat and the splashes of footsteps growing smaller and passing into a curtain of rain.

No, no, no.

Instinctively he leapt to his feet and ran after her, but he'd lost her. It was like the first moment he'd seen her, chasing her through the fog. She was a ghost, passing through realms of invisibility. The sky was getting heavier with rain, and thick, black clouds had blotted out the moon entirely. It didn't look real. But it was.

He could hear voices but wasn't sure of their direction. He walked cautiously forward, toward where he imagined the middle of the field to be. Briefly he looked back, wishing he'd told Bradley to hide behind the trees, but he was already too far away to see him. Everything was a blur.

He was cold, but his trembling was from the fear. And then, he saw them and froze entirely.

Beatrice looked so tiny before her father, who towered over her, all chest and shoulders, thick muscle and girth.

Jason could hear them. Through the rain, he could hear her voice.

"No," she said. "No."

"You belong at home," Tereus said.

"I don't have a home here," she said.

"You have a home with me."

"No. It was never a real home. Not to me."

It felt like slow motion. A great arm rose into the air, a fist like a great stone formed at the end. And Jason didn't think. He ran full speed.

He thudded into Tereus. It was not strong enough to knock the man down, but he stumbled sideways, his arm dropping roughly to his side.

Beatrice backed away as Jason regained his footing. He looked up into the molten face of a monster.

"How many of you are there?" Tereus said with a snarl.

Jason wanted to run. But he knew he was now the only thing standing between Tereus and his friends.

"Are you the tough guy now?"

Jason remembered the knife. He had slid it through his belt, hooked at the hilt. He fumbled with it, expecting Tereus to jump at him at any moment. But the man just watched him, bemused.

Finally, it was free. Jason held it up, his hand still shaking. Tereus laughed.

Jason took a step back.

"You know what?" Tereus said. "I'm going to kill you with that."

And then the man was charging. Jason didn't have time to do anything with the knife before Tereus launched a knee into his stomach and he keeled over, wheezing. Tereus was still laughing.

But Jason hadn't dropped the knife. It was his only hope of surviving.

He pushed himself back against the ground, his heels kicking up a wall of mud in his wake.

Tereus moved again toward him, slower this time, leaving enough of an opportunity for Jason to rise to his feet. As the man ran at him, he swung the knife wildly in front of him. It cut Tereus across the forearm, but he was entirely unbothered and completed his tackle.

Tereus was on top of Jason now, a mountain falling on frail bones. The boy was pinned, squirming. He felt as if he might suffocate. And then, there was relief, but only for a moment. Tereus rose to his feet, grasping Jason in his arms, pinning Jason's side to his own. Jason held the knife limply in his wet hand, but it began to slip out.

Tereus shook him, jumping up and slamming him down. Jason's brain rattled against his skull, and he saw stars, then a blip of blackness. When he regained his senses, he realized that the knife was not in his hand anymore.

Tereus released him. He instantly fell to the ground again.

"It will be fun killing you," Tereus said. "But not as much fun as it was your friend. He was stronger."

Jason swept his arms wildly around on the ground, feeling for the knife, but all he could grab was wet grass. He could hear Beatrice crying close by, but he couldn't see her.

Tereus reached down and grabbed his ankle, but Jason kicked free. He scooted backward in desperation and winced when he felt the point of the knife stick him in the back. It was under him. The man was quickly approaching again, as he felt underneath him to grab the handle. Swinging it out from under him, he cut himself in the back but now held the blade out in front of him, pointed at Tereus.

Jason jumped to his feet, but he was no match. In half a second, Tereus had a hold of his forearm. Jason thought his arm might break. Tereus grabbed his knife-holding fist with his free hand and easily pried it loose. They both looked at the blade, now rising in the man's grasp—Jason with horror and Tereus with delight.

Jason turned to run, but time was speeding up, and he was slowing down. He felt a sharp pain in his right hip, a searing cut that drove down the length of his leg and set the nerves in his foot on fire. He instantly stopped, stumbled, grabbed for his hip. He felt the grip of the knife. It was stuck in him at a vertical angle, all the way to the hilt. Apparently, Tereus had stuck it in him before he'd even begun running.

Jason felt woozy. Shock began to take over. His right leg was going numb.

Then Tereus was grabbing him again, holding him in a terrible bear hug and squeezing.

Jason felt the tension in his ribs, his bones stretching against the pressure. And then he couldn't breathe.

No.

He looked up, and the face of Tereus, burned red, all scars and hatred, was grimacing in strength. He looked up beyond him to the sky.

No, he thought.

His eyes fluttered, and as he opened his mouth to suck in more air, Tereus squeezed harder, and he felt as though he'd be shattered to bits, exploded into nothingness, just blood and bones to be scattered across the rocky shore below.

I didn't want this.

I know.

Why does it have to be this kind of story?

I hear you.

I think I'm going.

No. It's not over.

I think this is it.

I see you.

I miss my family.

I know. But I'm here. I see you.

Why like this?

Jason.

Who? Who is that?

I'm with you. I see you.

What was happening? He was delirious. Hearing voices. Getting close to the end. Jack said the first death was just the beginning. He'd already been through that. And this was definitely worse. The second death.

When you die here, you really die.

And he couldn't let it end that way. If he was going to die, he wasn't going to die this way.

A reservoir of strength surged through him. A last-ditch effort at survival, bewildered and wild, absorbed him. While he could not burst the bonds of his monstrous captor, he lowered his head and buried his face into Tereus's vulnerable chest. And then, he bit him at the heart.

Tereus yelped and instantly dropped the boy.

Jason fell to the ground, still gasping for air, his lungs filling and burning with oxygen. His chest felt sunken, his arms broken, his legs soft. He couldn't move.

And then Tereus was on him again, standing over him with all the rage of hell in him. He brought a booted foot down into Jason's stomach, and the boy jerked sideways, retching into the grass.

The boot was on his turned head now, pressing him into the ground.

Tereus was going to crush his skull.

And he would have done it much quicker if the ground hadn't been so soft.

Jason's face sunk into the wet grass. The danger now was not his head breaking under Tereus's foot but his mouth and nose filling with mud. He would drown.

Beatrice was at Tereus's back now, raining a series of inconsequential blows upon him. He didn't even turn to brush her off. She couldn't stop him.

Then, as Jason's head finally hit upon something solid, a stone beneath the field perhaps, he was in danger of being crushed again. His hands flailed for purchase, and he found it—the knife still stuck in his hip, pinned now between his leg and the ground.

Jason pulled the knife out, slipping it from muscle and fat like Excalibur from the stone. And as he felt his skull about to crack, with his remaining strength, he thrust the blade into the ankle of his tormenter.

Tereus screamed, stumbled, grabbing at the knife stuck firmly through the muscle. He tottered as he gripped it, and yanked it out only to scream again, step backward, and then . . . over the edge.

He was gone.

Beatrice rushed up to Jason.

He was swallowing big gulps of air.

"What—what," he gasped.

"Jason," she said.

"What. Where is he?"

"The cliff."

The pain disappeared for the moment. He rolled over and looked behind him. He was mere feet from the edge of the fields, the overlook to the ocean, and he hadn't even realized it.

They found Bradley where they'd left him. Jason collapsed at his side, startling his friend, who had passed out.

"Wh—what," Bradley said. "Is . . . is he here yet?"

"Yes," Jason said. "He *was* here. It's over."

Bradley lifted his head slightly. "You're alive."

"Yeah," Jason grinned. "We're alive."

Bradley smiled. "I knew you had it in you."

"No, you didn't."

"You're right. I didn't."

Jason laughed. He put a hand on Bradley's shoulder and squeezed.

The rain had stopped, and the clouds were breaking, scattered by the dawn, which rose in pink and orange and turned even the gusty winds into a gentle breeze.

Beatrice stood over them, her face resolute.

Bradley looked up at her, then again at his friend. "Here we are," he said.

"Yeah," said Jason. "Here we are."

17

HOME

Jason and Beatrice were drying out by the fire in the cabin, hunched over in a row along the hearth, as Jack puttered away at his desk. He was putting the finishing touches on a passage in one of the green notebooks. Jason gently stroked his injured hip, now tightly bandaged.

Nobody spoke.

Bradley was sleeping in the corner, his arm in a makeshift sling. Though his face looked like it had been through a meat grinder, it was oddly peaceful. He was snoring.

Jason looked across the cabin, so strange and sparse. *Was this always here?* he thought.

Jack lifted his pen to his lips, from which he'd just removed his pipe, deep in thought. He tamped the pipe into the ashtray, set it down, and then returned to writing.

The sun was shining so bright outside; there was no need of a lamp inside.

Then they heard it. For the first time since the whole story began, they heard the sound of life. A sweet, flirty chirping of a bird. And then there he was at the window, a sparrow perched on whisper-thin legs on the sill, his sliver of a beak twitching this way and that as he peered inside the glass.

Beatrice looked at the bird, blank-faced, then she reached over and took Jason's hand. He held hers on his knee.

No one wanted to break the guide's concentration, as if it might undo the whole story and ruin the ending.

Minutes passed. They watched the bird watching them and chirping.

And then, Jack put his pen down and closed the green notebook. He leaned over in his chair and slipped it in at the very end of the bookcase. Then he just sat there, staring at the desk.

Jason finally spoke. "Is that it?"

Jack turned to face them. He leaned back, crossed his leg. "Very nearly," he said.

"And what's it all about?" Jason said.

"A story isn't so much what it's about," Jack replied, "but *how* it is about it."

"I don't understand."

"Naturally. And that is part of the story too, you see. From the beginning, there's really only been a handful of stories. But a million ways to tell them. But I do think you did a smashing job with this one."

"*We* did? But we weren't writing it."

"Weren't you?"

"I don't know if you're joking."

"Only a bit," said Jack. "You could've stayed in that cave, you know. That could've been the end."

"I've thought about that," said Jason. He leaned back, feeling the warmth of the fire on his hips. The place where he'd been stabbed throbbed in the heat. "I could've stopped my part, I think. But I'm not the only character. It could've gone on with the others." He looked at Beatrice, who was still watching the bird.

"Oh, perhaps," said Jack. "But it was you who needed to get to the fields. The charge was for you, no other."

"I had a part to play," Jason said.

"*Have*," Jack corrected. "You have a part."

"Is that the story, then?" Jason asked. "Good versus evil, that sort of thing?"

"A good story isn't one thing, lad. But yes. Good versus evil, if you prefer. But there are readers right now, reading these very words, taking a bit of something else here and there for themselves. Like all myths, it may work elementally like that. One story that encompassed many."

"It's a love story," Beatrice suddenly said.

Jason looked at her again, but she was still staring at the window.

"Yes," Jack said. "Certainly. I think you feel that most keenly, don't you? But not the kind of love story many expect, or even desire. Not a romance in the modern sense. The great lover is indeed invisible to the plot."

Jason cocked his head, confused.

Jack said to him, "Consider that it was love that led you out of that cave. It is love that makes the story worth going along with, in the end. It was love that drove Bradley to Tim's side, and you to Bradley's. It was love that saved you in the battle. It is love that makes all the pain and toil worth it. And, I should add, it is the pain and toil that make the love real."

Bradley broke in then. He'd been listening. "What about Archer?" he asked. "We have to find him."

Jack frowned. "No, I don't think so. His part in the story is done. He could not cope with it, you see."

"But I know where he is. He's at his house, reading that notebook."

"No, I don't think so. Not at the moment. He is wandering. And he will be for quite some time. No, he cannot go on with you. I will remain here to help him should he ever recover, but he will not share the ending with you, I'm afraid."

"And how does it end?" Jason asked.

"I was only told until the previous chapter, and even that point only at the last moment. I did not know until then if you were to prevail through victory or through sacrifice. And from this point on, like you, I am but a character in discovery."

The bird flew away. Beatrice turned to Jack. "Is the world still gone?"

"Yes, dear," Jack said. "The world you knew, yes. Perhaps you could make the world anew in this place. The mystery of this island runs deep. There is much more to discover. But alas, not by the three of you. As for what is beyond, I do not know."

"I want to know," Jason said. "I want to know what else the Author has out there."

Beatrice now looked at Jason. What he'd said set off a spark inside her chest, warming her all over, far more than the fire at her back. She released his hand and lifted her arm to link it with his. "So do I," she said.

Bradley shifted nervously. "Um, you guys wouldn't leave me behind, would you?"

Jason grinned at him.

"I mean," Bradley said, "love story or whatever."

Jason limped over to the corner and gave his friend a hug.

Soon they were at the ferry landing, the sun at noon position in the sky, a halo over their procession.

"The sailboat, I think," Bradley said.

"No," said Jason. "We should row."

"It's the ocean, man."

"I know. We should row."

Bradley shrugged.

There was a rowboat in the shallows, and Beatrice was already onboard, sitting atop a tiny perch in the stern. Bradley steadied it in the gently lapping waves.

Jack stood nearby, puffing on his pipe, overseeing the proceedings.

"Here," Jason said to Bradley. "I've got it. Watch your hand."

Bradley clambered in and settled portside, taking up the oar in his left hand, his right arm pinned against him in the sling, his shriveled hand in his lap.

Jason held the boat steady. To Jack he said, "So you really aren't coming?"

"No," Jack said. "I must remain."

"But you have to come with us. We don't know what's out there. What if we need you?"

"You have what you need for the next part. And I cannot go with you anyhow. Beatrice will lead your way from here."

"But what if everything's really gone? What if there's nothing out there, and the island is all there is?"

"Then you will discover that. But if there is more, if there is another world out there, you won't know unless you go, don't you see?"

Then they heard it again. A low moan rolling in from the horizon, carried by the wind and waves.

"There's something out there," Beatrice said.

"What if it's not safe?" said Jason.

"What if it's not?" she said with a glimmer in her eye.

And then, without another word, they were rolling out to sea. Jack grew small behind them. When they'd cut through the breakers, they turned westward, circling the southern part of the island until they couldn't see land anymore at all.

Jason on the right, Bradley on the left, they rowed steadily into the eternal horizon.

Beatrice sat up in the stern, elevated and beaming, her blue dress gleaming in the sun and rippling in the wind. Her hair flew in a long trail behind her. There were more birds suddenly, gulls swooping down into the water around them, the gentle waves yielding their feed and glistening in the sunlight as if they bore on their ceaseless currents an infinite field of diamonds.

She was queen of the sea.

The boys were her courtiers, rowing and rowing, fueled by the future and its suddenly boundless possibilities. Scared but together, they were smiling big smiles now, and the sun had never felt so warm on their faces.

They were rowing to the immense edge of the unknowable world, the great hearth of that new earth, the end of a page they could not read.

Jason looked up and beheld Beatrice as she stared off into the sky, her face fearless and free. She was the most beautiful thing he'd ever seen, and he thought to himself if he must plunge off the end of the world, down some vast waterfall into the void of outer space, out of this world and into another or into nothing at all, he'd gladly do so with her. She was worth it. It had all been worth it.

But it was more than that, greater. He felt born. He felt new. He felt oddly and splendidly, finally, himself.

Was it a dream? A story? Something else entirely? Something for which he had no words and no knowledge? It didn't matter.

The boys rode the writing, cranking their strong arms, each stroke a turning of a page, willing the rushing to the end.

Jason faced the blank line where the island used to be, the end of that story, and he rowed backward with Beatrice as his eyes. Beatrice was now his guide, the beacon of some beatific vision still ahead.

There is more to see.

Jason looked up now, up and out to the sky that overlooked, as far as he knew, a big blank world. He looked all the way up.

I see you. I cannot see your face, but I see you. Don't put down the pen just yet. I have energy left and more to see, further to go.

I know. I see. You will not fall at the end of it all. Keep rowing.

And he did. He kept rowing.

NOTES

1. Dante Alighieri, *The Divine Comedy*, II, 53–54.
2. C. S. Lewis, *Perelandra* (New York: Macmillan, 1965), 201.

ACKNOWLEDGMENTS

This story is the product of stories upon stories. Many were read to me as a child, many more were read by me—on school buses, in waiting rooms, behind textbooks in class, and under the covers at night with a flashlight.

I am grateful for the teachers along the way who nurtured my draw toward stories and gave me good stories that both satisfied me and stirred the hunger all the more. When I was in the fifth grade, Mrs. Larke introduced me to both Middle Earth and Lake Wobegon. In the seventh, Mrs. Dosher let me read *Les Misérables*. In high school, Mrs. Woolley foisted Faulkner upon me and set me free to write and write and write without apology.

A select few authors are more responsible for this tale than the wide world of others who are only generally so. Astute readers will recognize the scattering of mythology throughout, and cast over the entire novel are, of course, the shadows of Dante Alighieri, George MacDonald, and C. S. Lewis. I trust the latter will forgive me in the world to come for the liberties I have taken with his character here. But it felt right for him to serve

Echo Island as MacDonald served *The Great Divorce* and as Virgil served Dante's *The Divine Comedy*.

Many thanks are due to all the kind folks at B&H and B&H Kids for their helpful guidance in and support for this story, including Michelle Freeman and especially editor Anna Sargeant, who asked a million annoying-in-the-moment questions that served to make the story stronger and clearer, as all good editors are good at doing.

I am grateful also for the friends (like Bill Roberts) who read the first part of this story fifteen years ago and waited all this time for the rest of it. And for my wife, Becky, who did the same.

Mostly I am grateful for the real Author of the true Story and for the incarnate Word. Because of Him, we need not fear pushing out to sea, even if the clouds are foreboding and the waves rough. He is able to stride upon them.

Don't be afraid; keep rowing.

ABOUT THE AUTHOR

Jared C. Wilson has been obsessed with stories since before he could read. In grade school, he wrote a work of short fiction, stapled the pages together, and tried to sell the product to classmates. Numerous teachers cultivated his love for storytelling over the years. After graduating from Middle Tennessee State University with a bachelor of arts in English, he landed a literary agent with his first novel.

Today, Wilson serves as the Author in Residence at Midwestern Seminary and as a professor at Spurgeon College, Midwestern's undergraduate school, where he teaches pastoral ministry and writing. He has authored over twenty books. *Echo Island* is his second novel.

Wilson lives outside of Kansas City, Missouri, with his wife, Becky. They have two teenage daughters and a teenage dog named after Indiana Jones (who was himself named after a dog).